NO MORE HORSES:
Vet in a Muddle!

'How come we've got a foal?' Tim asked Sara.

'I went to the Sales,' Sara said miserably.

'And you found an old mare with a foal and they were both going for horsemeat,' he said.

'Yes,' said Sara. 'I know I promised; but you should see the mare; she's not that old, she's half Arab and if she weren't starvation thin she'd be so pretty; and she's quite good breeding and the foal's sweet.'

'And you got it for nothing, thrown in with the mare. How old is it?' Tim asked.

'It was born before she was due to go into the Sale; nobody realised she was in foal,' Sara said.

'I sometimes wonder if people are born blind,' Tim said and irritation sharpened his voice.

Tim had been working for a whole year as a vet but he still couldn't believe how badly some animals were treated. It made his blood boil, and he knew he would have done the same as Sara. The only trouble was, where were they going to find the money to look after them. They really must be no more horses . . . .

NO MORE HORSES:
Vet in a Muddle!

Joyce Stranger

Carousel Books
Transworld Publishers Ltd.

NO MORE HORSES: VET IN A MUDDLE

A CAROUSEL BOOK 0 552 52168 X

First published in Great Britain in 1982

PRINTING HISTORY
Carousel edition published 1982

Carousel Books are published by
Transworld Publishers Ltd.
Century House,
61–63 Uxbridge Road,
Ealing, London W.5.

Printed in Great Britain by
Hunt Barnard Printing Ltd., Aylesbury, Bucks.

NO MORE HORSES:
Vet in a Muddle!

Contents

Major Characters

Tim Yorke: newly qualified veterinary surgeon.
(Timothy Ivan Neil Yorke, known to his friends as Tiny because of his initials).

Mr. Fitzpatrick: his employer, known to everyone as Fitz.

Mrs. Fitzpatrick: known to everyone as Mrs. Fitz.

Lisa Matthews: animal nurse

Tamsin: animal nurse

Sheila Grant: secretary and receptionist

Aunt Dora: Tim's aunt who breeds standard poodles.

Meg: the new vet.

Tim's dogs:

Zia: a standard poodle given to him by Aunt Dora as a present.

Dana: a rescued collie cross that he took on when no-one else wanted it.

Tim as a child often stayed with an uncle who bred horses. The uncle is now dead, but his knowledge helped Tim to decide his future career.

1

There was a cake on the table in the office, and the three women were grinning as Tim walked in, an hour before the evening surgery. Sheila Grant, the receptionist, was wearing a skirt and blouse; dressed for an occasion, with a gold chain at her throat. Tamsin Leigh, although in jeans, was wearing a brilliantly coloured Fairisle jersey that set off her thick dark hair and dark eyes while Lisa Matthews, the other nurse, had an air of triumph about her, and had added a gold brooch to her daily working trousers and short white jacket.

Tim looked at the cake.

It was decorated, iced, and bore one blue candle. Someone had lovingly and rather untidily piped words on to it.

'To Tiny Tim, our Gentle Giant on his first anniversary.'

'Honestly,' Tim said, laughing. 'You are a lot of nuts.'

'Bet you forgot you'd been here a year,' Tamsin said, handing him a cup of coffee, while Sheila cut a huge slice of cake. Fitz, their employer, came in to the office while she was cutting it, looked at the cake and grinned.

'Your parents should have thought a lot harder before labelling you with the initials T.I.N.Y.,' he said. 'There's a letter from your mother.'

He handed it over and Tim looked at the address.

T.I.N.Yorke, Esq. His mother never had understood why he objected to his initials, yet she could so easily have named him Timothy Neil Ivan, which wouldn't have been half the problem, especially as at twenty five he was lean, and broad shouldered and topped six foot three inches and was anything but tiny.

'Mothers are given us as crosses to bear, I sometimes think,' Fitz said, correctly reading Tim's expression. 'Mine always referred to me as her Cherub; and in front of my school friends; you can imagine what it did for my image to go through my school years labelled 'Mummy's cherub.' I could cheerfully have killed her on a number of occasions, especially when I left school aged eighteen with a face more like a demon than a cherub. I've improved with age,' he added, seeing Tamsin's glance at Lisa.

Lisa grinned.

'I don't know what that's supposed to mean, young lady,' Fitz said, his mouth full of cake. 'And I won't ask. Where ignorance is bliss . . . this is a very good cake. Who's the culprit?'

'I made it and Lisa iced it,' Sheila said.

'And Tim's a year older, a year wiser and has almost become a real vet,' Fitz said. 'Feel as if you've been here a year, Tim?'

'It feels more like a hundred years,' Tim said with some feeling. 'All made up of twenty four hour days. I'm beginning to wonder if there's a conspiracy among the local cows to stop me sleeping. I've been to four calvings this week; all starting at 2 in the morning; all needing ropes; all on days when I'm taking morning surgery.'

'It's the pigs that are keeping me up,' Fitz said.

Tamsin laughed.

'You should see our files with that new smallholding you've been going to,' she said. 'Their sows' names are unbelievable; there's Swallow, Nightingale, Willowtit, and Peahen.'

'I should think Peahen started the naming,' Fitz said. 'She screams more like a peahen than a sow. And she has agonies over nothing; I've never come across a sow quite like her. A proper prima donna.'

'That's because they keep them more like dogs than pigs,' Tim said. 'I went out there one day and found one of the children leading Peahen round on a rope, and giving her titbits; those chocolate drops you give dogs!'

Fitz finished his cake and held his plate out for a second slice.

'My birthday is on November 7th,' he said to nobody in particular. 'This is a very good cake.'

Lisa winked at Sheila.

'Message understood,' she said.

'I wasn't hinting,' Fitz said.

Everybody laughed. It was a rare day with time to relax and time for once to spend together. Only Meg Ingram, the new assistant, was missing. She had been called out to an injured foal. She drove into the yard just as Sheila was cutting a piece of cake to set aside for her.

'Cake . . . super,' she said as she came into the room. 'Whose birthday is it?'

'Tim's been here a whole year,' Sheila said. 'So we thought we'd celebrate.'

Meg took her plate, broke off two corners of the cake, and handed a piece each to Tim's two dogs. Dana, the collie cross, was now a sleek little animal, more collie, with her black and white thick shining fur and prick ears, than anything else. No-one was quite sure what else was in her. Zia, the Standard Poodle,

11

was now full grown, though not yet mature, a lovely bitch with a thick curly coat which Tim kept cut short.

'I won't ever show her in breed,' he said, looking at her now. 'I don't want to grow her show coat; it's not very practical for the sort of life she leads.'

'In and out the middens,' Meg said. 'She still stinks of pig; I don't think you washed her very thoroughly.'

'I hosed her,' Lisa said. 'And she's smothered in Apple Blossom talc as well but the smell of pig takes some removing.'

'I sometimes think I smell like a pig most of the time,' Fitz said, glancing at the appointments book. 'What's Battling Billy been up to now?'

Battling Billy was a large Siamese cat that lived with the delusion that the whole of twenty-four gardens belonged to him. Even cats that lived in the gardens were driven out. Nobody ever remembered his real name, which was Sebastian.

'He decided to take on an old stray that had moved into his territory,' Tim said. 'The result was an ugly bite between the ears that has abscessed. He's coming in to have the abscess cleaned out and I think I'll have to remove all the skin and muscle down to the bone; it's one of those rotten puncture wounds that goes deep.'

'Are we keeping him in?' Tamsin asked.

'I said we would; his owner has just had a new baby and he would add to her work load,' Tim said. He spoke with feeling, having just spent a week with his older sister and her brand new son, who seemed to occupy more hours than there were available in any day. It was quite a relief to leave the baby and come back to work, even if it did involve getting up in the middle of the night to a calving cow four times in one week.

'That will be fun,' Lisa said with considerably more feeling than Meg felt was needed.

12

'What's wrong with the poor cat apart from his injury?' she asked.

'You wait till he's here; he has the loudest wail I've ever heard, even from a Siamese,' Fitz said. 'He'll say over and over again at the top of his voice "I want to go home" and if we don't listen he'll say it louder.'

'He's gorgeous, though,' Lisa said. 'He's the most beautiful colour, with black mask and black legs and black tail and the rest of his fur is toffee coloured except on his front which is cream. What's more he knows he's gorgeous and he poses.'

'Sounds as if we're in for a noisy few days,' Tim said. 'I'm glad the hospital is out of earshot of the cottages.'

The ringing phone interrupted them. Lisa swallowed the last crumbs of her cake, and moved to answer it.

'Sara,' she said, ringing off. 'She wants you to go over, Tim. The foal's in considerable pain; she thinks it's colic.'

'She hasn't got a foal. You must have misheard,' Tim said. He and Sara were partners in the stables a few kilometres away. Sara had been going to sell up when Tim offered to go into business with her after winning a thousand pounds on Ernie. He soon realised a thousand pounds wasn't anywhere near enough nor ever would be, but he couldn't let Sara down. They had begun to buy in ponies for Sara to school and sell to children as riding ponies. There certainly weren't any foals. They had sold the last foal a few weeks before.

'It's urgent, anyway,' Lisa said.

'I'll operate on Battling Billy if he comes in on time,' Fitz said. He scribbled R. Fitzpatrick across the bottom of a cheque that Lisa was holding out to him and went to check the operating room, whistling under his breath. He loved operating. Tim preferred to be out in the fields with the farm animals and the horses, or to

13

have dogs and cats with only minor injuries.

Tim drove out into the lane. It was a sunny day for once, and he felt light hearted after the party. It was good of the girls to make him a cake and it was a super cake. Lisa had cut him a huge piece to take to Sara, who was now almost part of the practice as she often drove down in the evening after surgery to talk about the stables with Tim. Tim had his own horse at the stables. Hawk was a handsome animal and Tim took immense pride in him but he rarely had time to ride.

'Get down, girl,' he said to Zia who had stuck her nose into the back of his neck. She obeyed at once. Dog club was paying off, he thought. Dana never moved once she was in the Land Rover, and curled up into a black and white ball, her coat shining. Her tail wagged at the sound of his voice, but she moved nothing else.

Sara was waiting at the gate. Her long hair was tied back in a pony tail and she wore her usual working uniform of breeches, wellingtons, and an old and rather tattered anorak.

'How come we have a foal?' Tim asked.

Sara looked at him.

'I know that look. What have you done?'

'I went to the Sales,' Sara said miserably. Tim looked at her, one eyebrow cocked. Anyone else would have wondered why such a simple statement should be made in such an unhappy voice, but Tim was beginning to know his partner only too well.

'And you found an old mare with a foal and they were both going for horse meat,' he said.

'Yes,' Sara said. 'I know I promised; but you should see the mare; she's not that old, she's half Arab and if she weren't starvation thin she'd be so pretty; and she's quite good breeding and the foal's sweet.'

'And you got it for nothing, thrown in with the mare. How old is it?' Tim asked.

'It was born just before she was due to go into the Sale; nobody realised she was in foal,' Sara said. 'The vet saw her and removed her.'

'I sometimes wonder if people are born blind,' Tim said. Irritation sharpened his voice. Six months ago he might have lost his temper, but he was learning to keep his red-head passions under control. It was never easy. Sara looked up at him doubtfully, half expecting an explosion. They were finding it hard to keep the horses well enough as it was, and Tim was putting more of his salary than he had intended into financing the business.

'I've a new horse at livery,' Sara said. 'Full livery; which will help with the feed bills for two months. The owner has had to go abroad on business. He's a darling. A twelve year old bay, with the nicest manners.' She patted the dark nose that strayed towards her over the stable door. Tim stopped to look and to breathe softly into the horse's nostrils. He never could resist a horse.

'Let's see the worst,' he said, with a final pat.

'His name's Robot,' Sara said. 'It's a stupid name; he's far from being a Robot so I've rechristened him Robbie which suits him much better.'

The bay had turned to reach his haynet.

'At least he's in good shape,' Tim said. 'I hope this mare of yours isn't too rundown.' He was aware Sara was deliberately delaying him.

He missed the glance that Sara gave him. Had he seen it he might have been very worried indeed.

She turned towards the foaling box in the far corner of the yard.

'I've isolated her,' she said. 'She's not very happy at all, and I don't think she's ever been in a stable before. She's been kept rough. I led the foal in and she followed and since she's not in the best of shape . . .' she stopped talking as she saw Tim's expression of total disbelief.

'She couldn't go for horse meat; there isn't much on her anyway and they were only bidding twenty pounds, I got her for twenty two. The knacker said she wasn't even worth throwing to the hounds.' Sara stood looking at her latest purchase.

Tim looked at the mare too.

'There are times when I hate people,' he said. 'Who owned her? Do you know?'

'Somebody bought her for a riding pony. She was left out too long and they never had time for her. They tried to school her too late but she'd developed all sorts of bad habits. She won't come when she's called and she hates the girth being tightened and tries to bite. She doesn't like people behind her and she kicks and she kicks other horses so they left her alone. Then they got fed up with her and decided to sell her.'

'So she's had one rotten life,' Tim said. 'Is she trusting at all?'

'Not really. She hates me near the foal, but I can lead her out, I think, so that you can examine it. It's only about twenty four hours old.'

'And as weak as a kitten; it will probably die on you. Sara, look at her. Think of all the signs of good health; horse alert; well she isn't, she's as miserable as can be; head up; it's down. Ears pricked. She isn't even listening to us talking; she's away in some world of her own. Eyes bright; look at them, and look at the corners of them; they've never been cleaned in her life by the look of her; they're a disgrace. Her skin looks like old rope; her mane and tail are coarse and harsh and need grooming; her feet need trimming. Has the blacksmith ever been near her, I wonder? She's some milk but not much. Has the foal sucked?'

'I held him up to her twice since they came home,' Sara said. 'He is sucking but not very well. I have to milk her, into his mouth and help him, and I have to tie her up very firmly and take care.'

'Have you been kicked?' Tim asked. He thought he had detected a certain amount of pain in Sara's movements.

She nodded.

'Tim . . .'

'You know she ought really to be put down out of pure kindness,' Tim said. 'It's crazy, Sara . . . she's going to be a full time job. She needs teaching to trust people; she needs feeding up. She needs a lot of care; those eyes are going to need bathing three or four times a day and she not only needs building up but you will have an awful job to get her fit.'

'She's pretty,' Sara said. 'Look at her. Imagine her with flesh on her and in good shape; she's very pretty.'

The little mare was a skewbald; chestnut and white, with a tail carriage that betrayed Arab ancestry.

She was well shaped, and as she bent her head to nose her foal and the foal lifted his head and whickered softly to her, her expression changed. She tried to nudge him to his feet. He stood on wobbly legs and collapsed again.

'He isn't strong,' Sara said.

She moved forward and at once the mare's head swung towards her, as if she were going to bite.

'Steady, girl,' Tim said softly.

'The foal's got a temperature, or I'm a talking parrot,' Tim said, after a few minutes more thoughtful inspection. 'You'll have to get the mare away. I'll give him an injection. As to her, give her some food, but be careful; if she isn't used to stable rations it might upset her. There's not any reason why she shouldn't be put out to graze while it's warm enough.'

'She'll have to be put in the paddock by herself,' Sara said. 'I didn't really think about the work involved. I just couldn't leave her for meat. I hate the thought of people eating horseflesh; or even dogs eating it.'

'I can't say I'm keen,' Tim said. 'Look I'll go in and make some tea; Lisa's sent you some of my anniversary cake. Then you can get the mare away from the foal on your own; it might be easier than having someone else around. How long has she been here?'

'About three hours,' Sara said. 'She'd travelled for the first time for years to the Sale and kicked the box almost to pieces; they had to do all kinds of things to her to get her in, the owners told me; they haven't a clue about horses. The worst part of it is they don't know they haven't a clue. I hope they don't buy another.'

'Where did she foal?'

'In a barn behind the sale yard; luckily the vet there noticed at once that she'd started and they took her away from the other horses and put her alone among the cattle, in a pen in a corner. She was in an awful state and nobody even gave her a bran mash after; just some hay.'

Tim went inside, leaving Sara to go across to the foaling box. He wasn't at all happy but he couldn't see that either of them had any choice and what was more, he knew very well that if he had been at the Sale he would have probably done the same thing. It didn't do to be soft hearted; he was always regretting his impulses. He poured the boiling water on to the tea bags, and put out Sara's cake. The mare was whinnying to her foal and the foal was answering. He would have to go out and examine it thoroughly and be quick about it or she might well try and jump the paddock gate and come charging in on him and he had no doubt whatever that she might bite, or kick.

The foal was even thinner than its mother. He looked down at it, wondering if it would last the night. Sara watched him as he examined it. He didn't like one thing about it and became more and more unhappy. It was skin and bone and nothing more; the mare had obviously not had enough food while she was carrying it, and it was also riddled with worms. It twitched one ear, and nuzzled his hand.

He filled the syringe and injected it.

'Anti-biotic and I hope it works,' he said. 'I haven't a clue what's really wrong; and it's been born a bit early which won't help at all. And I suppose you don't know if the mare has cleansed and got rid of the afterbirth, or if the foal has had its first bowel movement; we're working blind.'

'She's cleansed. Paul Simon was the vet and I had a word with him; he was with her when it happened and he's quite positive about that. As to the foal, I only know nothing's happened since it came here. I doubt if it would have fed much anyway travelling.'

Tim was busy examining under the foal's tail.

'I think it's probably OK,' he said. 'Watch it; we don't want a stoppage on our hands and the poor mite can't stand up to much in the way of treatment; he's only a tiny hold on life. I don't even promise he'll make tomorrow. Put his mother back and come and have some tea.'

Sara ate the cake to please Tim, but hardly tasted it. She wished she had never gone to the Sale. She wished she had never seen the mare, but she knew very well that once she had seen her one thing after another had to happen; she had no choice. There was no way she could have slept at night if she hadn't tried to save the two.

Tim glanced into the foaling box just before he drove away. The mare was standing, pulling gently at the haynet. She upset him even more when he saw her revealed by the last rays of the sun, her ribs showing, her skin almost paper thin, and the crusts round her eyes still in need of removing. Sara was going to have a job on her hands. He gave her a lotion for the mare's eyes.

'You won't do it,' he said.

The mare dropped beside her foal and the baby cuddled up close against her. Her eyes looked at him dreamily and her neck stretched protectively across him.

'Prepared to bet?' Sara asked.

Tim shook his head.

'I reckon I need to take a second job to keep her and her foal,' he said.

He climbed into the Land Rover, to be greeted ecstatically by both dogs. He had been dimly aware at one point that both were howling mournfully because he was so long gone.

'Tim?' Sara's voice was uncertain.

He looked down at her.

'Are you very mad at me?'

'I'd probably have done the same myself, but please, Sara, don't go to any more Sales till we've got these two on their feet,' he said. He smiled at her. 'No, I'm not mad. I don't think I'd like you much if you'd just left her to be turned into meat.'

He drove home, the setting sun low on the windscreen, dazzling his eyes. He had to concentrate on his driving, but he was aware all the time of a small nagging worry. He saw no way in which the foal could possibly survive and he wondered just what would happen to the mare when the baby died. She had very little strength herself and life had treated her badly.

Fitz was due to take evening surgery. Tim glanced in but didn't want to talk to the girls. He walked to his cottage, aware of a strange and unlikely noise that he realised must be the loud complaints of Battling Billy waiting for his operation.

There was another noise that was even less identifiable coming from the little stall where they housed sick farm animals. Curious, he walked across and looked inside, to find himself gazing into the wise yellow eyes of a white nanny goat busy suckling two newborn kids.

He watched for a few minutes, delighting in their strength and health. They made a sharp contrast to the mother and son that Sara was nursing in her stable. It was nice to know there were some owners who could do a magnificent job.

'Little Shelly Markham's experiment,' Meg said as she came across with feed for the new mother. 'Do you remember her? She's just twelve and had always hankered for a nanny goat and they gave her one for her last birthday; almost a year ago now. On condition she did everything herself. She joined the goatkeepers club and I gather she's beginning to know a great deal about goats. You can't beat that for good condition can you?'

Zia and Dana were butting at his knee. It was feeding time. He nodded to Meg who wondered at his sudden curtness. He took the dogs indoors. The nagging worry about the foal had returned. He was Sara's partner and it was as much his foal as hers.

They shouldn't have rescued the mare, and they were going to lose her anyway.

He determined to set his alarm very early and go up and look at the mare and foal first thing in the morning. Meanwhile the dogs needed food and needed excercise, and he suddenly remembered it was club night and he had promised to help with the puppy class and play at being a vet for the new pups. There were six of them. A beagle, a German Shepherd, two little collies, both black and white and almost indistinguishable from one another as they were brother and sister, a Great Dane that was going to grow enormously in the next few weeks and a fluffy yellow golden retriever with fur that reminded him of a chick's down. She was all wag and wiggle and licking tongue and it would be a good thing to go and forget his new worries for a while. He felt much lighter in heart as he drove down to the club.

2

It was difficult to realise that a year ago, he had been a newcomer to the dog club, Tim thought, as he swung the Land Rover into the car park behind the building. He had known a great deal about sick dogs and how to cure them and surprisingly little about dogs as animals. They were all so different.

He was now part of the teaching group, and puppy owners were coming as a matter of course to the nursery class, knowing their vet helped to take it. Many people were afraid that puppies would be taught to work like the older dogs and were reluctant to bring them, so that it was always suggested that people came and watched first.

Once they had watched, many of them were only too eager to start.

'Quiet, dogs,' Tim said to Zia and Dana, who were whining eagerly, wanting their turn to come. They had to stay in the Land Rover while Tim helped with the pups, a part of the evening he found tremendous fun. There were rarely more than three little ones at a time.

'Hi,' he said, as he walked into the hall. Tamsin had already put out the apparatus, which was intended to help the puppies get used to strange objects in their surroundings, and not to be afraid, whatever might happen. The modern dog could meet anything on his travels from a JCB to an armchair dumped in the ditch, and also had to get used to all kinds of noises.

People grinned at him. Tamsin lifted a hand and went on putting out various items on the floor. A kettle; a lamp-shade; a cushion, two tiny jumps, made of bamboo sticks covered in red and white insulating tape, balanced on flower pots; a tunnel made from a large cardboard box, a couple of chairs draped with an old groundsheet, which made an obstacle for the puppy to walk round to find his master in a game of hide and seek.

Tim now made a point of getting to club whenever there were no emergencies. Even Fitz had to admit that the pups that came to the classes were far easier to manage than those that didn't, as Tim regularly examined them, as a game. It was much more fun examining healthy puppies than sick ones that he always felt sorry for and wished he could wave a magic wand and heal in a few minutes.

'No newcomers tonight so far,' Tamsin said, sitting down at the table and checking off the money in the books. 'Just the three from last week; the Dobermann's six months old and he's gone up; he's coming on a treat.'

Dane the Dobermann was a happy outgoing dog with a stub tail that never stopped wagging; his black and tan coat gleamed with health, his eyes sparkled and though he occasionally played the fool and tried to swing on his lead or roll on his back when he should have been lying quietly on his front, he had made excellent progress.

The other three pups were all fourteen weeks old. Sheba, a ball of golden fluff, was the little golden retriever bitch, who was plainly going to have a mind of her own. She was extremely intelligent and again an outgoing animal, with a gleam of mischief in her eye, and the certain knowledge that she could twist every human round her paws with one melting expression.

Tara was a spaniel, and Tim was less happy about her, as her first owner had been in the Army and suddenly and unexpectedly posted abroad so that Tara had already had two homes in six weeks, and was plainly very uncertain about life. Her present owner had only had her for ten days, and had never had a dog before. She was an elderly lady who had recently lost her husband and everything worried her, including the puppy. Also the pup hadn't met other dogs or people other than her owners and was afraid of everything. She lay under one of the chairs, her eyes frightened.

The third pup was only a problem in that he was a small black labrador that appeared to have about ten times as much energy as any other pup in the hall. Blue bounced in at the end of his lead, barking, and Tamsin quieted him at once by picking him up and playing with him to distract him.

'Tara's your responsibility,' Tamsin said in a whisper. 'I think Mrs Smith will take what the vet has to say a little better than she will from the rest of us. For goodness sake don't let the puppy lurk like that; she must come out and mix, but it isn't going to be easy. She's terrified.'

One of the most difficult things was going to be his own height, Tim thought ruefully as he walked across the floor. Mrs Smith was a tiny woman and the pup was a scrap of a thing. He sat down on the floor beside the chair and held out a hand for the puppy to sniff. She retreated even further under the chair.

'She does that all the time at home,' her owner said.

'She's got to come out and mix,' Tim said. 'If she doesn't now she never will and you'll have a dog you can't take anywhere. Come on, sunshine, out to Uncle and don't be a silly girl.'

Tamsin, passing, hid a smile. A year ago Tim would

never have dreamed of talking to a puppy like that. He'd come a long way, she thought, as she went over to show the labrador's owner how to calm him down. It was much easier if they each could take a new owner, as the pups really all needed such different treatment at first. Once they had learned to be calm, or not to be afraid, and all behaved like normal little dogs, then the real training could begin. It often took ten or twelve weeks to get rid of odd habits and then only if the owner worked hard during the week.

Tim might have been reading Tamsin's thoughts.

He had pulled the pup out from the wall and was cuddling her against him, glad that Fitz had given her her preventive inoculations and that she didn't associate him with the needles that pricked her. Sometimes it took several sessions for one of the pups he had inoculated to realise he wasn't going to do it again, but it was worth doing as when they did need treatment they came in happily, knowing Tim well and he could examine them without any fear on their part at all.

He tickled Tara's black and white chest, and rubbed his nose against her cheek. He had tiny pieces of baked liver in his pocket, a trick that Tamsin had shown him, and he held out a piece now. The pup was too edgy to touch it. He left it on his hand and ignored her, talking to her owner.

'She needs to be put on her lead, even indoors and brought to meet all your friends,' Tim said.

'Nobody visits,' Mrs Smith said. 'We'd only just moved here when my husband died and I haven't had time to meet people yet.'

'Right,' Tim said, thinking fast. 'Then perhaps we can fix it for Tamsin to drop in briefly as she drives home; and I can call for a few minutes when I pass; you live at Rosemary Cottage, don't you? The pretty little cottage on Lamb Lane.'

Mrs Smith nodded, her face happier. Tim suddenly realised how lonely she was and that she needed company as much as the pup. Maybe she would make friends among other people at the dog club later on; at the moment Tara was too frightened of the other pups.

A newcomer walked into the hall and Tim looked up and his face lightened. Janet Grey had left her dog in the car and come in before her class to help with the books. She came with a neighbour who always took her big Wolfhound for a long walk before bringing him in to train, to try and get some of his energy out of him. He was a beautiful dog, but extremely active, even for his breed. Janet was only just sixteen but she was very sensible.

And what was more, so was her dog.

'Jan,' Tim called.

She came across the room, a small girl, not yet more than five feet high, with a mass of bright chestnut curls that tumbled to her shoulders. Blue eyes looked at him. She had never quite conquered her awe of Tim as a vet.

'Can you bring Misty in and let her sit beside this pup? She's lovely with babies, isn't she?'

'She'd adore that,' Janet said. 'She'd steal puppies if she could. It's a shame that she lost hers and had to be spayed.'

Misty was a handsome German Shepherd bitch, with a beautiful black and gold coat, a creamy chest, dense fur on her tail and under her tail, who walked in regally beside her owner.

Mrs Smith looked at Tim, her eyes worried.

'I don't much like Alsatians,' she said.

Tim laughed.

'There are as many bad spaniels as there are bad Alsatians,' he said. 'You get bad dogs in all breeds. Not many. The odd one or two. You only hear about the bad ones; no one ever writes much about the good dogs, but Misty is super. Janet's training her for Working Trials, so she tracks and searches; and she adores puppies. Just watch her.'

He turned towards the big bitch.

'Look, Misty. Puppy!' he said.

Misty already knew. Her head came forward and she nosed the tiny spaniel gently.

'Down, Misty,' Janet said, and the big bitch dropped to the ground, put her head over Tim's arm and looked up at him with an adoring expression.

'Misty and I know one another well,' Tim said. 'She had a lot of trouble when she had puppies; the puppies died; we don't quite know why, and she went septic afterwards and had to have an emergency operation to save her life, late on a Sunday evening. She nearly died too so she stayed in hospital for a week as Jan's mother goes out to work and Jan was at school. I did all Misty's dressings and we got to know one another really well, didn't we, girl?'

Misty licked his cheek and then turned her attention back to the puppy. Tim laid it gently against the Alsatian's warm body, and Misty licked it from head to toe. Within a few minutes it had relaxed.

'I think that will be all we'll do with her for today,' Tim said. 'She's had a lot to put up with really, poor baby. First a house full of children for a few weeks, and then suddenly quite a different sort of home, before she'd even had time to settle into the first. Jan, would you have time to call in with Misty for a week after school and let her and the pup get to know one another?'

'Of course,' Janet said. 'I'd be glad to, if her owner doesn't mind.'

'I'd be delighted to see you, my dear,' Mrs Smith said, and looked as if she meant it. 'I've a grand-

28

daughter about your age, but she lives in Australia now and I do miss her. I don't know many young people any more.'

'Time for the next class,' Tamsin said.

'Come and sit at the back with me and Misty and let Tara lie on the floor with Misty,' Janet said to Mrs Smith. 'We have coffee in about half an hour. You don't have to rush home, do you?'

Tim went out to fetch Dana, and Tamsin followed him.

'Tim, Janet's leaving school, and looking for a job. Lisa's going to have a baby in seven months time; don't tell her I told you, but Jan's asking Fitz for a job; I think she'd be good, don't you? We could do with someone extra as Sheila isn't getting enough time off. Would you back me up?'

'Of course,' Tim said. 'Watching her just now I thought how sensible she is and she's thoughtful as well. Most girls would be anxious to get away from an elderly lady, but Janet took it for granted that she would help us, and she'd done a wonderful job on Misty.'

'It's lovely to get the good owners, and see the pups come on,' Tamsin said.

Dana leaped from the car into Tim's arms, hurled herself at him to be put on her slip chain and then heeled perfectly beside him, when he told her, into the hall. The agility class had already started and he lined up for his turn. Dana adored jumping and went over the hurdles like a cat, slid through the tunnel, emerging to bark and raced without being told for the box where Tim put her down fast, or she'd have done it without being told.

He heeled her through the slalom poles and took her to sit in the corner, but not too near the little spaniel as Dana was sometimes too eager with pups and that would certainly alarm this one. Dana wanted to play and could never understand any dog that didn't want to play with her. That had once earned her a bite on the nose but even that hadn't cured her.

Zia was in the last class, and now in the display team. Dana, tired by her efforts, curled up at once in the Land Rover, nose tucked under her tail and went to sleep. Zia danced out, in her show off mood, trotting into hall like a hackney pony, making everyone laugh. Pleased with the result of her efforts she stood on her hind legs and pawed the air.

'Behave, you nut,' Tim said, no longer embarrassed by anything this clown of a bitch could do to him. He had learned in the past six months to laugh at himself as well as her. He took his place in the line and was thankful that Zia settled to work on her part of a complicated figure of eight heeling routine that involved as many changes of place as a country dance. Tim sometimes wondered if Tamsin had worked it out from an old country dance. He made the last elaborate move and got shouted at.

'Tim, that's Sally's place, and Sally's got herself in Joe's place; what's up with you three? Everyone else got it right.'

'Had a tough day,' Tim said.

'Haven't we all. Once more and then coffee.'

Once more turned into three times more as the end group muddled their places. Tim's group stood looking pious and earned a glare from Tamsin.

'I need my coffee,' Joe said feelingly, as he patted his large yellow Labrador, Leo, on the the head. 'Both need it, don't we, lad?'

Leo's tail wagged and Tamsin grinned as Joe took one of the saucers and shared his drink with his dog. Sally, having tied her Dalmatian, Bryn, to the pipes at the end of the room, helped herself to a chocolate biscuit, put her money in the Guide Dog tin, and went to talk to Mrs Smith and admire Tara, who was beginning to wag her tail, just the tip of it, when people spoke to her.

'A few more nights like this and Tara will be a normal happy little dog,' Tim said, watching.

'What's more, I think his owner will be happier too. She's a bit shy and it's not more than four months since her husband died; she needs socialising as much as her dog does.'

Tim leaned against the table, his thoughts drifting away from the club to the stables on the hills and the little foal and mare that Sara had landed herself with. If only it survived that night they might have a chance. And if not Sara would be unhappy for weeks. She was far too soft hearted.

'Penny for them,' Joe said.

'Just work,' Tim answered, a little blankly, not wanting to share his thoughts.

'You want to watch it,' Joe said. He was as tall as Tim and much broader, and worked in an insurance office, a job that didn't seem to suit him a bit. Tim had expected him to be a security guard or some other form of outdoor work.

Tim had just finished his coffee when there was a squeal of brakes from outside, a rending crash and the sudden keening of a dog.

'I hope that's not one of ours,' he said, and rushed through the door. Tamsin grabbed the first aid box and followed him.

The car had skidded into a lamppost. The driver was standing beside it, while his passenger knelt over a small black dog that Tim had never seen in his life before.

'He just ran across the road,' the woman said, sobbing. 'My husband swerved, but we couldn't miss him.

He was chasing a cat. Bob braked when he saw the cat; that got away.'

'I saw what happened,' said a woman nearby. 'I was waiting for my bus, but I'm not in a hurry. Would you like me to come with you to report to the police? Mr Yorke's a vet and Tamsin is one of the nurses so the dog's in good hands and you can't do anything; your wife's a bit shocked. I'm a nurse too. Maybe you can drive me home when we've been to the police and come in for a coffee. I don't think your car is too badly damaged. Has the dog a collar and disc on him?'

Tim shook his head.

'Probably a stray. I think we can save him if we operate. I'll drive up to the surgery and you can bring him, Tam. It'll be more comfortable in your car than mine and you haven't a dog with you. My two would probably go spare if I add an injured animal to my cargo.'

Joe had followed them out.

'I'll take over in club and lock up,' he said.

Tim, driving back through the dark, the hedges outlined in his headlights, wondered if it was sensible to operate on the dog: it might be better to put it to sleep. It hadn't been in good shape even before it was run over. Nobody's dog. And it was never easy to find a home for a dog like that and no way could any of the practice take on another animal. They all had more waifs than they ought. He had rescued Dana. He thought briefly of Aunt Dora, who had given him Zia at eight weeks old, hoping he would show her, breed from her and win prizes with her. He didn't want to show in Breed. He would work her and what was more, in Working trials, as he had become fascinated by tracking and Zia adored searching. Only it took so much time for teaching the dog and he never seemed to have enough time.

Joe had already telephoned to Lisa and the operating theatre was ready when they arrived, Lisa herself waiting to give the anaesthetic. Tamsin was just behind him. She carried the little dog in. He lay, watching them with terrified eyes, aware of pain and not much else, of strangers. His life up to now had been that of a scavenger, feeding as best he could on rubbish thrown out by people who had more food than they could eat; chased off by those who didn't want him in their gardens or near their dogs, living under sheds, hunting for warmth and longing for company, which neither dog nor man had given him. He didn't much like people or dogs.

He whimpered and Tim patted his nose.

'All right, old fellow. We'll fix you up,' he said. The dog licked his hand, pleasure at the first gentle voice he'd ever heard briefly overcoming pain. Tim injected him and in a few minutes he was unconscious. Tim began to work, so intent on what he was doing that he did not realise Fitz had come into the room, having seen the operating room lights from his bedroom window as he went upstairs to bed.

Tim put in the final stitch, and looked down at his patient.

'I'll take him home and he can sleep in a box beside my bed,' Lisa said. 'I'm a light sleeper. Poor little devil, he doesn't look as if he's had much of a life up to now. Look at his eyes and his ears.'

'And his fleas, Lisa,' Fitz said. 'Put him in the hospital, but spray him first. You can't have him in the house like that. He's been running wild all his life, I'd reckon. Who's paying for this lot, Tim?'

Tim looked at Tamsin.

'Our charity box,' Tamsin said firmly. She had recently started a fund at the dog club to feed rescued dogs and cats.

'Come on, sunshine,' Tim said to the unconscious dog and lifted him and carried him into the hospital and put him down on newspaper in one of the big cages. The Siamese, who had had his head operation, woke and began to shout at the dog. A small spaniel in one of the lower cages came to the wire, his tail wagging and tried to nose Tim's leg. Tim bent down and scratched the little dog's head.

'What's up with him?' he asked.

'He's a large cyst on his leg. I'm removing it first thing tomorrow. The owners went to a wedding today so I promised we'd keep him here overnight. They were getting back too late to bring him in first thing tomorrow and we've a heavy list for the rest of the month without taking on extra. That stray dog's not becoming part of this practice. If you cure him and he's fit to be owned and not run amok all his life, then he has to have a proper home. I mean that. I know you lot.'

'We haven't taken on that many strays,' Lisa said indignantly.

Fitz yawned.

'If we don't go to bed none of us will be up in the morning,' he said. 'It's nearly one o'clock. That husband of yours will be divorcing you, Lisa.'

'That husband of hers will be walloping her. This is no time for a future mother to be out of her bed. I told her not to come.' Mark was standing in the doorway, having decided it was high time his wife came home.

'And I told you not to tell them,' Lisa said.

'I think that calls for a celebratory cup of coffee, or at least cocoa to help us all sleep,' Fitz said.

'And the rest of Tim's cake. I'm starving,' Tamsin said.

'You'd better sleep on my spare bed.' Lisa had plugged the kettle in and her husband was sitting

34

inspecting a hole in his bedroom slippers as if he had never seen a toe before. 'Luckily your parents are used to your emergencies. It's too late to drive home now.'

It was a longstanding arrangement. Tamsin's father was a cripple and her mother not very fit, but a neighbour always looked in on them when Tamsin was out. She would get up early and drive home and see that all was well.

While they were drinking their cocoa Meg appeared, trousers and jersey put on hastily over her pyjamas.

'Something wrong?' she asked. 'It's terribly late.'

'Lisa's having a baby,' Tim said.

'What, now?'

Everybody laughed.

'Wake up, love,' Mark Matthews said. 'In the fullness of time, which is about seven months away. It sort of slipped out, and Fitz decided to celebrate; being late and everyone having to get up early, we are all drinking cocoa. Like some?'

'Now I'm here, I might as well,' Meg said. 'That Siamese woke me; he does have a lot too much to say for himself.'

'Think of living with him,' Lisa said.

'I suppose I need a replacement for you,' Fitz said to Lisa as Meg walked over to the window seat and sat down.

'I'd like to come back afterwards; and to work as long as I can,' Lisa said. 'But we could do with extra help anyway.'

'Tim and I know a girl who'd do very well. She's leaving school at Christmas and wants a job with animals,' Tamsin said.

'So you and Tim have already fixed it all up,' Fitz said.

'No. We did discuss it though, tonight. She's a

35

remarkably nice girl.'

'I'll think about it. And now I am going to bed. This seems to have been two days instead of one. I sometimes wonder who does run this practice.'

'Sheila does,' Tamsin said, when the door had closed behind him. 'But I don't think Fitz notices. If it weren't for her we'd muddle the books and muddle the appointments and none of us would ever be where we ought to be.'

Tim picked a large piece of icing off the cake and ate it.

'It's my cake,' he said to the accusing eyes around him. 'I'm going to bed.' He looked at the telephone on the desk. 'And if you ring, I'll cut your cord in half!'

'Which would ensure we all lost our jobs,' Lisa said as she slipped her hand into her husband's and they followed Tim across the moonlit yard to the pair of cottages that stood side by side beyond the stone walled garden.

3

Tim woke to the sound of Dana whimpering softly. Both dogs knew better than to bark. He looked at the clock. What on earth was the matter with her? He rubbed his eyes, looked again, leaped out of bed, grabbing his clothes as she ran downstairs. No time to visit Sara and look at the mare. He'd forgotten to set his alarm and it was almost surgery time. There were already two cars in the gravelled drive outside the waiting room door.

Two biscuits; one for Dana and one for Zia. He held them up to show them and opened the door to the garden, first checking through the dining room window to make sure the gate was shut. The last thing he wanted was two lost dogs.

Both knew the biscuits were waiting and raced in as soon as they'd emptied, sitting looking up at Tim, their eyes pleading.

'Nicely,' he said, and both bitches nosed his hand and took the food gently. He had perfected cooking breakfast to a fine art and cut his slice of toast to put in the toaster while he shaved. An egg into the pan to poach, and by the time he was dressed, toast and egg were ready and the kettle was boiling. It meant bolting the food down, but Lisa would have rung him on the internal telephone system if there had been anything urgent waiting for him. Another minute or two wouldn't hurt anyone.

'Don't dare ring,' he said to the phone. Dana looked anxious; all she had understood was don't dare and she wasn't sure that she hadn't been about to do something wrong. Tim saw her expression and laughed.

'Not you, goof,' he said, which was enough to launch both bitches at him, tails wagging, trying to lick his ears in delight because he had at last spoken to them.

'In your next lives, belong to someone who isn't a vet and who has more time for you,' he said, patting Zia on the head. 'You do like being nurdled, don't you?' he added, using the absurd word that Tamsin had invented one day to describe the hard patting on her crown that Zia so adored. Dana liked her chest being tickled, very gently, with a finger tip, while she sat and looked blissful.

'Into the office with you both,' Tim said, and opened the door. The bitches followed him to the gate, waited while he opened it and trotted across the yard at his heels. A car drove in, passing him, and both dogs sat as Tim flicked his finger. Tamsin, watching through the window, smiled to herself. Tim had been a good pupil and it was all her doing. She had to be hard on him at first; he didn't always think and was sometimes too casual, but as the pups grew they had both gone through an extremely exasperating and naughty phase and Tim had soon realised that either he trained them, or life was highly unpleasant and that with his job, they would have to go, as no one had time for badly behaved dogs in the office. They couldn't be left in the cottage, as they wailed like airraid sirens and Mrs Fitz sent angry messages to him. She didn't like animals. If he didn't train them either the dogs went or he did.

Training had to be done and Tamsin helped whenever she could.

Now they were far from perfect but they were sensible, and did do as they were told and could be trusted to curl up quietly if everyone were busy.

'Bed, dogs,' Tim said, pointing to their rug, which was against the radiator by the big window, well out of everyone's way. Dana trotted across and looked at him to see if he would change his mind. Zia knew better and sighed deeply as she lay down, looking at him reproachfully, and then at the inviting garden that she could just see through the panes. The big window was very low in the wall.

'Problems?' Tim asked, buttoning on his white coat. Fitz had recently decided they would all look far more business like if they all wore the same uniform. Tim found his a nuisance as he was so broad that it had been impossible to find one that wasn't tight under the arms. He felt as if he were putting on a straitjacket.

'Makes me as ratty as old Hodge's goat,' Tim said, wondering if he was actually being stopped from breathing.

Tamsin laughed.

Old Hodge's goat was named Lucifer, and his favourite habit was to butt anyone who came within yards of him, though he gave them ample warning by standing on his hindlegs in the sideways stance that goats always adopted when they reared.

'Forget the thing,' Tamsin said. 'I'll see if I can get you a bigger white coat next time I go into town. Fitz had to go to a calving; and Sara phoned. Can you get in touch with the Foal Bank? That mare still has very little milk.'

That job would have to wait till surgery ended. Tim checked himself in the mirror. Had he done his hair? He'd totally forgotten in the rush. He combed it swiftly, slicking it back in place. He now wore it much shorter and very well cut and Tamsin, looking across again at him, thought what a difference the year had made. His grey flannels were neatly pressed, and the round necked sweater was of a far more discreet colour than the brightly jazzed affairs he had worn at first.

Tim, unaware of her glance at him, went into the surgery, and waited for the first dog.

He checked the cupboard to see that he had everything he needed and almost went flat as two huge paws landed on his shoulders. He turned round fast.

'Major, you old demon!'

The enormous black Newfoundland grinned as if he knew he had been funny. His tail swept the day book on to the floor. His owner looked like a small tug being towed by a liner.

'What's he done this time?' Tim asked, solemnly accepting the vast paw that was now being thrust at him. Major had long ago decided that his role in life, like Zia's, was that of a clown.

'Actually, I don't think he's shaking paws this time,' his owner said. 'He's got a thorn in that paw. He's showing it to you.'

Tim very much doubted that the dog was, especially when after careful examination the paw proved to be thorn free and so did the other front paw. The left hind paw was a different matter. The thorn was a long one and had gone in deep.

'It will hurt, so don't eat me, will you, fellow?' Tim asked, as he knelt with the forceps to try and pull the spear-like object out without breaking it. 'This is going to be tricky, so keep still.'

'Stay,' Major's owner said. Major, who was part of the dog club and who, when the club collected for the Guide Dog it was buying, wore a harness with a collecting box on it, stood rock still.

'If only all my patients were like you,' Tim said.

'Daft dog,' he added, as a vast tongue swept across his face. 'How can I see to take your thorn out if you drown me and blind me?'

Major's tail threatened to come off.

'Sorry, it does make a draught,' his owner apologised, as Tim stood up, holding the thorn to the light, and grinned delightedly as he had taken it out whole.

'I'll give you a powder to dust it with, and give him an injection,' Tim said. 'With luck it will heal without any problems. Also bathe it three times a day with Epsom salt solution. How long's it been in?'

'Only this morning; he started limping as soon as he picked it up and kept trying to nudge me and show me; we weren't far from home, in the little wood, so it was a slow journey back. The milkman gave us a lift in the end.'

That must have been quite a sight, Tim thought, as he inserted the needle and pushed down the plunger. Major watched him with enormous brown eyes, aware that this was for his own good. He was nearly seven years old and in his life had had so many odd accidents that he took a visit to surgery as part of his normal routine. Sheila felt sorry for his owners every time she made out the bills.

'Nice easy one,' Tim said, as the dog went out. 'What's next? Not something tricky I hope. I ate my breakfast too fast and it feels like a lump in my midriff; it's all I can think about at present.'

The tiny dog that pranced in was a total contrast to Major. Tim laughed.

'From giants to midgets and all my old friends,' he said. The little papillon was all character and had the ideas of a very large dog in his very small body. He was a regular prize winner at the big shows, and remarkably valuable for his size, though that didn't matter much to his owner, as he was also her house pet and slept in a little scarlet box lined with white, beside her bed.

'What's wrong with Solly?' Tim asked. The dog's

show name was Solomon the Emperor, but it was always shortened at home.

'He's coughing slightly. I just wanted him checked as there's a show on Saturday and I can't take him if he's infectious.'

Tim sounded the little dog thoroughly and then opened his mouth and looked down his throat. Solly, like Major, was a dog club member and stood still.

He was also used to being examined thoroughly by judges, though they didn't peer quite so far down his throat, but Tamsin did, every Tuesday night, to make sure that none of the pups made a fuss when taken to the vet for examination.

Tim adjusted the light so that it shone into the little dog's mouth.

'He's got something stuck in his palate. It looks like a fish bone,' he said. 'Has he had fish?'

'No. Hang on, he was at the bit bucket yesterday and I'd thrown away some fish bits after filleting the fish. And his tummy is a tiny bit upset today. He must have taken some of the raw fish. I thought I'd got him away in time.'

'He'd better stay in and we'll sedate him to take it out,' Tim said. 'It won't be too difficult. I think that's all that's making him cough. It should come out with the forceps without any problem and then he's got three days to recover before the show. Give him to Lisa, and tell her why as you go out.'

'You never know what they'll do next,' the owner said, as she went through the door.

'Trouble?' Tamsin asked, as Tim frowned as he made a note on the card.

'With Solly? No. Only a fishbone. Looks simple. I've still got indigestion,' Tim said. 'Next time I oversleep I'll have breakfast after surgery.'

'Like yesterday, when we never saw you all day?' Tamsin said.

There was a bark and a sudden snarl in the waiting room, and then the sounds of a fight. Tim and Tamsin almost collided in the doorway. Tamsin walked over to the two fighting dogs, a little terrier and a bigger spaniel. She grabbed the collars, and hung both in the air, struggling, before returning them to their owners.

'Sit well apart,' she said. 'And don't let them do that again. Or you'll have a bigger bill than you expected; and the one that started it pays for both lots of treatment.'

There was silence in the waiting room as she and Tim went back into the surgery.

'Both owners incite their dogs to fight,' Tamsin said. 'They think it funny. Other people don't. And sometimes people get bitten too.'

She held up a bleeding finger for inspection.

'Hazard of the trade,' Tim said.

'Unfeeling brute.' Tamsin was cutting a piece of gauze. She washed the injury under the tap and added the gauze, still wet, to the bleeding wound.

'That'll make it worse,' Tim said.

'That's the general idea. I'll stop it bleeding and see to it properly when the two dogs have gone. I intend to make it look far worse than it is and teach our young gentlemen a lesson. Don't be surprised at anything I do, will you?'

'I never am,' Tim said. He looked at her, his mouth twitching. 'Don't scream when I'm stitching a cut, will you?'

'I won't do anything daft,' Tamsin said. 'That's a promise.'

Lisa opened the door, saw Tamsin's remarkably bloody hand, which was now smeared all over, and raised an eyebrow.

'Don't always believe what you see,' Tim said.

'Like that, is it?' She called out the name of the

terrier owner, who came into the room, his dog dragging at the end of its lead, barking.

'Behave yourself, Spot,' the owner said. He was a tall fair lad, about sixteen years old, Tim guessed, and he was, he remembered, extremely cocky.

'He eats spaniels for breakfast,' the owner said.

'Not here, he doesn't,' Tim said, looking at the terrier, who had now bared his teeth and was looking back at Tim with an expression that did not make the dog look any pleasanter. He was one of the ugliest terriers Tim had seen, and had two battle scars on his shoulder.

'Muzzle,' Tamsin said, bringing over the bandages, which Tim whipped into place fast, and lifted the struggling animal on to the table.

Tamsin held out her bandaged hand, and looked at the owner.

'Your dog did that,' she said. 'Tim . . . I . . . think . . . I'm going to . . .' she slid to the floor. For one appalled moment Tim thought she really had fainted. There was more blood than he had realised. As he bent over her she opened her eyes and winked at him.

Tim thought quickly and went to the surgery door.

'Hold your dog still,' he told the terrier owner, who was looking extremely worried. Tim put his head into the waiting room.

'Is there any gentleman here with his wife?'

The request came out rather oddly, but a man in the corner said that his wife was with him.

'My nurse was very badly bitten stopping that fight just now,' Tim said. 'She's fainted. Could your wife hold your dog, and could you help me carry her into the office, where she can lie on the settee for a few minutes and one of the other nurses can attend to her?'

He looked round the room with satisfaction, seeing the looks on people's faces, and especially that on the face of the spaniel owner.

'It's not the dogs,' the man said, as Tim led him down the passage. 'It's those two lads . . . they coaxed them to have a go. Just at the age when they think it's clever. They're neighbours of ours. Dogs are nice enough during the day when they're both at school. Young devils, both of them, but the parents don't know what goes on. They're sly as well. You see things when you go about a lot with your own dog. Don't know what anyone can do, though.'

'Don't worry. This is laid on for their benefit,' Tim said. 'It isn't a bad bite, but Tamsin thought it time they were taught a lesson. The next one might be bad, and in fact if either dog comes with an adult, it behaves perfectly. Just don't let on when you come into the surgery, though.'

There were two doors to the office, and as Tim and his helper, who was an elderly man with a permanently worried expression on his face, helped Tamsin to her feet and half carried her outside, she whispered to them to go the long way round through the waiting room and make the most of it. Tim winked at his helper who grinned unexpectedly, and played his part nobly, going in with a very anxious look on his face indeed, saying just as they went through the office door.

'You don't think she'll have to have her finger amputated, do you, Mr Yorke?'

By now the mixture of blood and water presented a terrifying appearance and Tamsin's dangling hand had stained Tim's white coat, that he had grabbed and put on again, to add to the effect. Tim closed the office door as a series of gasps from Tamsin showed that she was about to laugh, and was no longer able to keep up the act.

She gave a great sobbing cry that made Zia bark.

'That was a gem of a remark to make,' she said, when she had recovered her breath, 'but I wish you'd warned me. I could see the spaniel owner's face. He's worried sick and serve him right, horrible little toad. It's OK, Sheila, it's all a big act. It's the Reeve boy with his terrier and the boy from the other side of the road with his spaniel; they both think it's clever to make the dogs hate one another, and set them on each other, being big and bold with tough dogs. I decided it was time they had a lesson. I did get bitten. It isn't bad, but I'd like some first aid please.'

'Lisa will take over,' Tim said.

'I'll be OK in a few minutes. Once it's bandaged the bleeding will stop,' Tamsin said. She smiled at the elderly man. 'You ought to go on the stage, Mr Prentice. That was quite a performance.'

'I didn't know I had it in me,' he said. 'It's time those two were taught a lesson. Glad I could help.'

Tim was relieved to find, when his ex-assistant came in, in his turn, that the elderly labrador only needed to have his claws clipped. It was treatment that he hated and it always took two people to hold him and a third to clip as his paws were ticklish. Tim patted the dog on the head when he'd finished and received a lick on the hand in reward.

'It wasn't so bad, sunshine, was it?' he said, and the dog wagged his tail, and walked out sedately beside his master.

'Tiffin was one of our first members at the dog club,' Tamsin said, coming into the room and similing at the dog's owner. She held up a plastered finger.

'It was only a nip,' she said. 'Nothing to worry about. Fitz came into the office while I was doing my dying duck act and wanted to know what was going on. He's added to the fun, as he went out and took both lads outside, told them their bills for treatment in future will be double, with such dangerous dogs and that if either attacks another dog, he will assume the dog was incited to attack and they will pay for the vet bills of any dog they injure, and pay double for that. Also if my finger is amputated he's going to get me to sue them.'

Fitz came back into the room.

'Sure it's only a nip?' he asked. 'Bites can turn nasty, especially if they go deep.'

'I'll keep an eye on it, I promise,' Tamsin said. 'And my anti tets are up to date.'

'They'd better be,' Fitz said. 'Tim, Sara called me to look at that expensive luxury she's just let herself be tempted into buying. The mare will have to be taken away from the foal and the foal sent to the Foal Bank. She not only hasn't the milk, but hasn't enough strength to rear a foal. She's in rotten shape, but Sara's right; if she can get her on her feet she'll be a nice little mare and in a few years might be able to have a really good foal. It's mainly undernourishment and neglect . . . a change from all these overstuffed ponies we're always seeing whose owners don't realise they are making them suffer by giving them as much food as a horse in full work. Can't get it into them that it's not kind to over feed.'

'Dog owners are like that, too,' Tim said. 'I had an old dog in this morning that is going to die four years before his time from pure overfeeding.'

'I wish we could do what the Americans do and get out individual diet charts for each dog,' Lisa said, shaking her head at Dana who had decided to try and steal Lisa's midmorning biscuit. Dana dropped to the floor, but her eyes watched every mouthful that Lisa took. 'Mind you,' she added, 'I can understand why they fall for it; look at that dog's expression.'

'Never been fed in her life,' Tim said.

'I gave Sara the phone number of the National Foal Bank a few minutes ago,' Fitz said, adding three spoonsful of sugar to his coffee, in spite of Sheila's accusing eyes. 'I know. I need to slim too, but I was up at three this morning, and I feel fragile; need some instant energy. Meg, can you operate this morning? I don't think I'm up to it. I'll do your visits instead.'

Meg nodded.

She was looking out of the window at the autumn garden where Mrs Fitz, elegant in cream baggy trousers, long black boots, and a royal blue anorak with a matching silk scarf tied over her head, was busy dead heading the dahlias. Meg wondered how she always managed to look so immaculate when everyone else, gardening, looked as if they had dressed themselves with clothes bought from a jumble sale. Although they had a part time gardener, Mrs Fitz loved to do her share.

The phone rang and Dana homed in on it like a pointer marking a bird. She was always convinced all people were deaf as they were so slow to get to the phone. She stood by it now, looking at them all eagerly, as if wondering who would answer it.

Tamsin reached out her arm.

Her expression changed and she began to make a quick note as she asked for an address.

'Whereabouts on the Brinton road?' she asked.

She rang off.

'Tim, a pony got out of a field, shied near a cattle grid, fell and she's lying under the grid; they're getting the farm people to move it but can you go down and help? They don't know if anything's broken; she could be in a terrible way and they're having a job keeping her from throwing herself around; they can't shift the grid without help. It's far too heavy.'

She handed him the torn off sheet from the pad with directions on it, and Tim was out of the door before the dogs even realised he had gone without them. He heard their voices raised in a keening wail of misery as he drove out of the yard.

4

Tim wished the Land Rover would go faster. Goodness knew what damage there was to the pony; he might have to put it·down and he would hate that. Cattle grids could cause dreadful injuries to animals. He remembered a horse that had broken three legs . . . but it was better not to remember that. He hooted impatiently at a milk van that suddenly swerved from one side of the road to the other to make a delivery and concentrated on his driving.

He knew the side road; it led to the entrance to the National Trust forest property and the grid was to keep animals in as well as out. To contain the deer and the sheep and the wild ponies. He had no time to notice the autumn trees, or the sweep of downland as he drove up the hill. He only had eyes for the little group of people, and the tractor that appeared to be ready to move. He grabbed his bag and leaped out of the Land Rover.

A man was kneeling on the ground, cradling the pony's head. She rolled her eyes, and tried to move her neck, but he held her firm.

'I don't think she's too bad; luckily she's a well handled sensible animal, and not too young; I've managed to calm her up to a point and prevent her from struggling too much. If you can hold her head for me, I can help them fix the ropes so that we can lift the grid off her. It seems to be resting on her; we might be lucky.'

Tim knelt down and began to talk to the pony. The grid seemed to be supported at one end by the gate, and to have missed her legs. Part of it rested on her hindquarters, but there was very little bleeding. If only she weren't injured internally.

'We've got a gang of men; it's safer than using the tractor,' the farmer said. He was a small man with a sour expression that was, Tim realised a moment later, due entirely to anxiety, as he bent to the little mare and spoke to her softly and smiled, lightening his whole face.

'Only a moment, my pretty. Don't you struggle now when we start to lift.'

The men worked as a team, shoulders under the grid, side by side on either side of the contraption. Gently, they moved together, easing it up, easing it away, until it lay clear of the pony. She struggled to stand, and the farmer and Tim helped her. The farmer led her forward. One easy step at a time, gently, gently.

Tim ran his hands down each leg.

'She's sound as a bell,' he said, giving an immense sigh of satisfaction and relief. 'Cuts, abrasions, a few lacerations; nothing that a bit of dressing and a little time won't heal. Have you a box for her?

'It's coming now,' the farmer said. 'Will you travel with her to my place? It's right off the beaten track. Nobody seems to know whose pony it is; I've a spare corner in the big barn that's warm and draught free, where I put new calves. I'll keep her till someone claims her. Can't leave her loose like this and don't know anyone else who has room for her. I breed the Speed-lock Shires. If no one claims her I'll keep her for my little granddaughter when she visits.'

Tim knew the big horses. He had often admired them at the various summer shows. They were black with white socks, with gleaming hides, and shining eyes, always beautifully turned out, and usually winning every prize available. The pony would probably be better off with him than her owner.

He stood beside her in the horse box, gentling her. She was a pretty animal, creamy in colouring and probably, he thought, almost pure Welsh Mountain pony; she might have a bit of Arab in her. She nuzzled his cheek, obviously well used to people and trusting them completely, which he guessed, was what had saved her from extremely bad injuries. That and the good luck of the right man happening along at the right time.

They turned off down a lane, and down a second lane. Tim had lost all sense of direction. He sat in the straw and talked to the pony whose ears moved in quick response. She looked down at him, and nuzzled him with her lips. She was beautifully mannered.

The farmhouse was old and had been built soon after Henry the Eighth had died, Tim guessed. It was built of mellowed brick, the roof thatched, the windows leaded. The yard was enormous, cobbled, and looked as if it was hosed down daily. The yard was surrounded by barns, vast affairs which would house dozens of beasts; and mountains of hay and straw and feed. Chickens pecked around the yard, and a bantam cock stood and shouted his defiance, the sun shining on his brilliant feathers and bright button eyes. A white pigeon flew over the yard and into a cote nearby.

Black Shire heads regarded them with interest as the ramp was put down for the pony to come out. She stepped out daintily. The farmer led her through to the corner of the barn, which was, Tim discovered, a miniature stable, divided into stalls. The floor was already thick with straw.

'One of my men came on and got it ready for her,'

the farmer said. 'It's the best wheat straw; I gathered it myself, and I'm fussy. Finicky George, they call me round here.' He laughed.

Tim suddenly remembered he had heard the name and the farmer grinned at him.

'I see it rings a bell,' he said.

Tim busied himself with the pony.

'Right,' he said. 'Standard treatment for shocked animal; I'll inject her, and can you watch her and call me if there's any sign of collapse? I don't think she has any internal bleeding; and she's not in too bad a state physically. All the same . . . shock can be delayed and she's had the very dickens of a fright as well as being pinned under that thing for some time and struggling. Lucky she hit the edge of it and flipped it up; happens once in a million times, I should think.'

'I hate grids,' the farmer said. 'They are useful but all kinds of animals get caught by them if they shy or run near them; I've known horses when hunting jump over them, coming on them without knowing they were there. Travelling fast it looks like an ordinary gap till you're nearly on it. I prefer a gate. More of a nuisance for drivers, but cars aren't the only things in the world.'

One of the men came in to the barn, carrying a bucket of water.

'I'll try her with a warm bran mash in a bit,' he said, 'if that's OK.' He put a haynet in place, and to everyone's surprise the little mare calmly turned her head and began to tug at it.

'She's a miracle. What a temperament,' the farmer said. 'I wouldn't mind buying her if the owner turns up. Susan's a bit windy on a pony and the other two grandchildren ride and jump. Sue would probably feel very happy on a mare like this.'

'Maybe no-one will claim her,' Tim said. He patted the soft muzzle. 'You are a pet, aren't you?'

'She's been handled too much to be unclaimed,' the farmer said. 'Somebody has worked on her and what's more, they've loved her. She thinks people are wonderful which means she's had a wonderful owner. Wonder how she came to be loose?'

Tim glanced at her. She was beautifully made, almost a show pony. The only thing he disliked was the way her fore-lock was cut in a straight fringe; it was a new fashion that seemed to be catching on and a great pity. Tim much preferred the tapered forelock which gave the pony a kinder expression.

Maybe though children didn't know how to do it.

'Phone for Mr Yorke,' someone called through a window and Tim ran.

'Tim?' It was Sara's voice. 'This foal will die . . . the mare has hardly any milk. I've rung the National Foaling Bank; Johanne Vardon . . . says we must bring it down at once. Can you come?'

'I'll be right over,' Tim said.

'Trouble?' asked the farmer.

'Mare with new foal and no milk,' Tim said, as he climbed into the Land Rover.

'You want the National Foaling Bank,' the farmer said. 'Wonderful organisation; used it myself several times.'

Tim nodded as he started the engine and put the vehicle into first gear. He drove out through the gates, hoping he could find his way to Sara's. The Shire horses were Fitz's patients and he had never been to this farm before although he knew the horses from the shows and he knew the name well.

'Can you ring and say we're starting,' Sara said, as he drove into her yard. 'Newport 811234. It's been engaged both times I've tried; I hope we can get through soon.'

'I'll try,' Tim said, picking up the code book. 'It's

Newport, Shropshire, isn't it?'

Sara nodded.

'It's Salop, in the code book,' she said.

Tim dialled and sighed with relief as he heard the ringing tone.

'Timothy Yorke here, veterinary surgeon,' he said. 'We've a mare with no milk and a new foal. Miss Vardon knows about it already.'

'I'll get Miss Vardon,' the voice said at the other end of the line, and Tim drummed with his fingers impatiently, but barely had time to count ten before a voice came on the line.

'How far away from us are you?' He liked the voice. It was pleasant and businesslike, the voice of someone who knew what she was talking about.

'A good two hours run, I'd think,' he said.

'Can you get the foal here?'

'Yes. Somehow,' Tim said, 'even if we have to get a hire car to do it.'

'Right. Then put it in a bran sack and tie the sack at the throat. Pad you car with straw, and be particularly careful to pad anything that the foal might hit if it struggles: like window handles and door handles. Get the owner to sit in the back seat with the foal across her lap, or at least its head on her lap. It's not a heavy horse foal is it?'

'No. Mare just over fourteen hands, I'd guess.'

'That's all you need to worry about for now. Getting here. We'll be busy while you drive.'

'Did you hear that?' Tim asked Sara who had been leaning against him, breathing in his ear. He had held the phone a little way from him in the hope she would hear.

'I'm off for a sack. But who will drive me? You can't get off, can you?'

'I'll see,' Tim said. 'We'll use your estate car if I can.'

54

He rang back to the surgery and was relieved to hear that Fitz was there. He explained the position, which Fitz had already guessed.

'OK. Meg and I can cope. But get back as fast as you can,' Fitz said. 'Lisa said she'll cope with the dogs, and not to worry about them. Good luck.'

'I've rung Sam . . . she's coming over to cope. Thank God she left work to get married and never got another job,' Sara said. She had a large sack over one arm. Samantha had been her partner until a year before, and it was Samantha leaving and taking her money out of the business that had left Sara in such a muddle that Tim had bought one of her horses and she kept it for him to ride; every penny helped in times like these.

'Sam should be here before we go.' Sara went to the stable and looked down at the foal. 'He has had some milk. Do you think she'll survive?'

Tim stooped to manoeuvre the tiny beast into the sack, and as he bent and put a hand on its hindquarters a small hoof lashed out and caught him on the shoulder. He gasped.

'It's nowhere near dead yet,' he said. 'I thought it would be much weaker. Teach me to be more careful.'

Fifteen minutes later they stood looking down at the little animal, at last securely trussed inside its sack. They had moved the mare into the next stall where she whickered for the baby and he called back to her, wanting her desperately.

'The mare's going to miss him,' Sara said.

'Only for a day or so,' Tim was lifting a bale of straw and carrying it out to Sara's estate car as he spoke. 'If you travelled on one of your floor cushions from the house you could be right beside the foal and might find it easier than putting the rear seat up,' he said.

'I'd already thought of that,' Sara said. 'We can pad the floor with straw. It's not so easy to pad the handles.'

'Cushions; and you lean against one. The lock is secure, isn't it?'

Sara nodded. 'Bale against the other side; straw on the floor; you're going to itch by the time we get there.'

A little blue mini drove into the yard and a dark haired girl jumped out.

'Carry on, and don't worry,' Sam said, pushing her long hair out of her eyes. 'I know what there is to do. Anything urgent waiting?'

'Only the mare in there; it's her foal. She needs feeding; and she could do with some sympathy too, I reckon,' Sara said.

She climbed into the back of the Land Rover and Tim brought out the foal. It remained quiet while in his arms, but as he laid it in the estate car it began to struggle again. Tim drove out of the yard, aware from the noises going on in the back and the mare's forlorn calls, that the foal was still answering.

It sounded as if there was a wrestling match going on behind him. He concentrated on the road ahead and tried to ignore the noises.

'I suppose you didn't think to bring a map?' he asked, when, after ten long never ending minutes, there was silence.

'It's asleep; exhausted, I guess,' Sara said. 'Yes, I did bring a map. If you reach into the pocket you'll find a motorway map there. Pass it back and I'll route us.'

Tim knew the route to the motorway. He was not sure where he left it or if the Foal Bank would be easy to find. He drove fast but very carefully, avoiding sudden braking or accelerating, in case the foal was bumped around and hurt itself.

'Tim,' Sara said, after an hour's silent driving, during which she had been busy with her own thoughts, and Tim had been watching the road, as there was a great deal of heavy traffic.

'Mmmm?' Tim pulled into the fast lane to overtake a line of freight lorries that appeared to be driving in convoy. He signalled and pulled across again.

'This is going to cost us, isn't it?'

'So?'

'So I'd better not go near any more Horse Sales,' Sara said.

Tim signalled and turned into the service station for petrol.

'I should think we could do with a coffee,' he said, and laughed. 'It's good experience for both of us and I'd like to see the Foal Bank; it's been on my list for some time. It's the only one in the world. I'll get us two coffees from the machine; you carry on baby sitting.'

He returned with two cups of coffee and two ham rolls, to find that the estate car was the centre of a ring of grinning lorry drivers.

'Do you always take the baby when you travel?' one of them asked.

Tim looked at him. He wasn't in the mood for jokes. He pulled out an envelope from his pocket.

Timothy Yorke, MRCVS.

He pointed to the letters. He hadn't time at the moment for fools.

'That means I'm a veterinary surgeon,' he said. 'The foal's lost its mother and we're taking it to the Foal Bank to get it a foster mother.'

'Valuable foal, mister?' one of the older men asked.

'Can't tell at that age, mate,' one of the other men said. 'The Foal Bank takes all sorts; racehorses, Shire horses, kids' ponies. They had a foal for my brother, did a grand job.'

The men drifted away.

The foal's eyes were open. It stared about it as if astounded by everything it saw, but it was used to Sara and to her scent, and felt safe cuddled against her. She soothed the soft neck, and it watched her with wide eyes.

The coffee was welcome. Neither of them had had much to eat during the early morning. Tim handed a slab of chocolate to Sara, and started the engine. The foal struggled briefly, but quieted more quickly than before, and once they were driving fast again, seemed to relax and enjoy the movement, reminding Sara of the way her tiny nephew always fell asleep fast when they wheeled him in his pram or rocked his cradle.

The Foal Bank proved easier to find than they had expected, and Tim was thankful to find they were expected.

'Mr Fitzpatrick rang to ask if you would hurry back and not look around today,' Miss Vardon said, as they lifted the foal from the car. 'We have a mare ready for your foal; and we'll get right on with it. You can ring tonight and see how they're doing. It doesn't look nearly as weak as some we get in, which is a good sign.'

Sara joined Tim in front of the car.

'Talk about straw in my hair,' she said. 'I've straw everywhere you can think of and some places you can't, and pins and needles; foals are heavy. They're a funny shape too when it comes to cuddling them, and I've a few bruises to show for our journey too. I'll be stiff tomorrow; those little hooves are surprisingly hard when they lash out!'

'At least you didn't get bitten,' Tim said, with vivid memories of taking an injured dog in his car when he was a student. He had found it lying in the road after being knocked over by a hit and run driver. The dog had been badly injured and terrified and whenever Tim had tried to touch him, had sunk his teeth in. It had died before they got back to the veterinary college, which seemed to Tim to be the final insult. It had been a lovely dog and should never have been out on its own.

'You're driving too fast,' Sara said. 'Calm down.'

'Sorry. I was remembering something I'd rather forget,' Tim said. 'Doesn't do.'

'Pull in at the next service station and we'll eat something and I'll drive the rest of the way home. No reason why we have to starve just to get you back to surgery, is there? I'm ravenous. And Sam's husband is away so she's staying a couple of days to help out. She sounded as if she'd like to come back again but I can't afford to pay her and can't expect her to work for nothing. Silly world, isn't it?'

'Very,' Tim said, pleased to see that the next service station was only seven kilometres away. He felt as if he hadn't eaten for a week. What was more, as far as he could remember it was one of the better restaurants. Some of them were awful.

They feasted on roast beef, yorkshire pudding, roast potatoes and peas and carrots, which Sara topped by a piece of Black Forest Gateau, while Tim, who preferred savoury food, found a very good Stilton and biscuits, spoiled by a pat of rancid butter which he changed for another equally rancid. The manager was apologetic, and brought half a pound of fresh butter from the sandwich counter.

Tim glanced at his watch.

'Somehow, I don't think I'm going to be popular today,' he said. 'Meg will have done the operating and surgery. Hope they haven't had any emergencies.'

It was a hope that seemed futile when at last he got back, and walked into what appeared to be a zoo. Tamsin, her white coat torn at the shoulder, was bandaging Meg's arm, while Lisa swept up glass and mopped the floor, and inside the office, Dana and Zia, hearing Tim's voice, yodelled as if they had been left on their own for ever.

The most extraordinary noise came from the hospital.

'What on earth's been going on?' Tim asked.

'Go and see,' Meg said. 'You won't believe it when you do see it.'

Tim walked into the hospital and looked at the cages. A large tabby cat that had come in to be neutered and was recovering from the anaesthetic; a dog with its leg in plaster, also not yet recovered from his operation; a small white bitch with four puppies that had come in the night before for a Caesarian as they couldn't be born normally and had to be cut out of her; and then he looked in the far cage. The small animal in it chattered at him hysterically and leaped around as if it were demented.

'Who in the world brought in a baby monkey, and what for?'

'You may well ask,' Tamsin said. 'It's a thousand times worse than that wretched magpie you had a few months ago. I've never been so relieved as I was when he was well enough to fly free.' Tim had been relieved too but he was the last to say so. Even now the bird occasionally visited them, flying in through an open window as if it still belonged, and several of the animals were terrified of it. Zia loathed it and fled, as the magpie tweaked lumps of fur out of her coat and delighted in it. Dana stood up to it and barked defiance which wasn't nearly so much fun.

'A sailor son brought it home as a pet for the family,' Lisa said. 'It's wrecked the house; bitten everybody; can't be housetrained, and it's pretty well gibbering mad; trouble is it's terrified; too young to leave its mother I suppose and it's proved so vicious everyone has been horrible to it. I don't know what we're going to do with it. It needs to learn people can be trusted; but it won't ever make a decent sort of pet and you can't housetrain them; and it stinks.'

The little animal had stopped yackering at Tim and

was hunched in the corner of its cage, sobbing like a baby.

'Poor little devil,' Tim said.

'Someone's got to feed that little devil with his bottle; and it's not going to be me,' Meg said. 'I tried; and it's pretty well bitten me to the bone.'

'How did they get it to England without milk?' Tim asked.

'They didn't. Someone had the mother as a pet; and she produced the baby on the way back; unfortunately she died two days ago; wrong feeding, I guess as they are fruit eaters and she'd been fed dog food. Or cat food; I don't know . . . people will take on animals and they never bother to find out a thing about them. Then when they die they blame us.'

'If I don't do something about my dogs, Mrs Fitz will be insisting we put them down,' Tim said, aware that the racket the two were making was getting louder and that they hadn't seen him all day and wanted to greet him. Dana had a shriek like a dying banshee and Zia, he knew, was sitting with her muzzle lifted to the ceiling, sounding like a demented foghorn.

'There's no more glass about,' Lisa said. 'That silly little object went berserk and rushed around throwing down everything it could put its tiny paws on and what it couldn't grab it shoved. You'd never think anything so small could do so much damage. You didn't see the worst of it.'

Tim laughed and went out and opened the office door; a moment later he was almost on the floor as Zia launched herself at him, crying and Dana raced round and round the waiting room like a dog possessed, her ears flat with delight, her tail going, crouching and herding him, leaping at his face trying to lick it.

'You ought to go to dog school,' Tamsin said, and as Tim fended Zia off for the forty fifth time, he turned and put out his tongue at her.

Mrs Fitz, walking in through the door to ask them to stop the noise which was making her head ache and driving her mad and not to be tolerated, was just in time to see him. She glared at him, and even the dogs were silent.

'I thought we employed adults,' she said, and the room temperature seemed to drop to freezing point. 'I expect you to behave properly at all times, and I will not have that appalling noise. I have never heard anything like today.'

She went out closing the door sharply behind her.

'She doesn't know she's born,' Lisa said, and then added, 'Tim, catch her,' as Meg suddenly slid off her chair on to the floor in a faint.

Fitz, coming into the room a few minutes later, found Meg on a chair with her head between her knees, while everyone else stood and looked at her, not quite sure what to do or what was wrong.

'What has been going on?' he asked. 'My wife seems to think you've been having some kind of mad tea party where everyone threw things at everyone else; and she also said that Tim put out his tongue at her.'

'I was putting it out at Tamsin or Lisa,' Tim said. 'Not sure who now; Mrs Fitz came in at a critical moment. It's been a bad day for everyone.'

'The Jenkins family were given a baby monkey,' Tamsin said.

'And it got loose and created mayhem. Well, that's one mystery solved; I knew there had to be a rational explanation. What's up with Meg?'

'It bit me,' Meg said. 'I think its teeth went in deeper than I realised; it's bitten me in the arm, the shoulder and the hand; and I felt faint.'

'She went out like a light,' Lisa said.

'I think we'll get you up to the hospital, young lady,'

Fitz said. 'I don't like bites of any kind; monkey bites don't happen often in this country and monkeys can have funny bugs on them. Let's be off. Get that foal sorted, Tim?'

'I think so. I have to phone later and see if the foster mother took him without any bother,' Tim said.

'Keep young Sara away from the Beast Sales or you'll both be bankrupt with that soft heart of hers; and I'm not sure about your head, young man.' He put an arm round Meg, who was by now feeling very odd indeed, and helped her out to his car.

'And now we need offers to give the monkey his bottle,' Tamsin said. 'No wonder they're called monkeys; they are monkeys.'

'I think you've got that the wrong way round,' Lisa said, looking thoughtfully at the feeding bottle that stood on the table, ready to be used.

'And now,' Tim said, 'just what do we do about this monkey?'

'Nothing at the moment,' Tamsin said. 'There's a queue outside and only one vet, and that's you.'

5

Fitz came into the surgery as Tim was making the last of his notes and Tamsin was marking up the book to keep the accounts straight.

'Meg's not too bad,' he said. 'Several bites that are nasty, but what none of us, including her, realised, is that she has flu. She's just starting and feels sick and shivery quite apart from being bitten by a monkey.'

'It's a long time since I had a human patient,' Lisa said, accepting at once that she would have to look after Meg. 'Is the flat warm enough?'

'I put the heating on. Meg's going to sleep. Maybe if you look in before you go home for the night she'll be able to tell you how she's feeling. Flu and monkey bites don't mix well, and I suppose we're all in for it.'

'There's a lot of it about,' Sheila said, and everyone laughed. No one quite knew when that sentence had become a surgery catch phrase but it was used for everything from spilling milk to road accidents and a glut of newborn kittens without homes.

'Let's look at that monkey,' Fitz said. 'I've had one or two to deal with in my time. I served my first two years after qualifying, in a Zoo; trouble with that is that you never know from one day to another what kind of patient you are getting and some of them aren't in any text books. Others present immense problems as there is no way you can get near them till they're out cold.'

The monkey was crouched at the back of the cage, glaring at them.

'To start with, he's not a baby; he's an adult and he wants food, not a bottle. Someone's been telling you a tara-diddle. Don't believe all you're told. He's a Capuchin monkey; they're small even when full grown. To go on with, I'd like to run round the streets of this country yelling don't bring monkeys in as pets; they don't make pets; they're wild animals and of all wild animals these are the most miserable kept away from their natural surroundings. They don't always take to humans; they might love them but they are just as likely to hate them, and they soon get bored and apathetic. This one's been through it all; he's been fed wrongly and he's losing his fur; he's been sitting in his own piddle and he's raw from it, as nobody has been able to handle him to clean him out, I'd guess. You can start by finding him a banana, Lisa. Most monkeys of his kind like those; and he can find out how to peel it if he's never seen one. It will give him something to think about, and take his mind off his miseries, and he's got plenty. He is feeling rotten, he's sore, and he's among total strangers; and he's had one hell of an afternoon, being chased around this place by you lot of louts.'

He saw Tamsin's expression, and smiled.

'I wasn't accusing you; I was just putting myself in his shoes. Look at you all, enormous giants, after one tiny animal that's terrified out of his wits.'

Lisa brought in a banana and the little monkey ran to the cage door and put his hand through, asking so plainly that they all stared at him.

'He knows about those,' Fitz said, and handed it to the animal who rushed to the back of his cage and turned his back, stripping off the skin till he could begin to eat and then eating as if he were never going to see food again in his life.

'I suppose some crook flogged that in a cage to the sailor lad, telling him it was a baby, and they tried to milk feed him afterwards. He's been away from his mother for a long long time. He's probably at least five years old. There ought to be a mass of fur on that funny little head; and he hasn't much anywhere else.'

'What are we going to do with him?' Tim asked.

'I remember a lady somewhere in Wales who's a wizard . . . or do I mean witch? . . . with monkeys. She's had them for years, and lectures on them; she rescues them from pet shops, from unsuitable homes, and takes in any that are born in a Zoo and neglected by the mother. I saw one of hers last year; he went to her at three days old, hardly big enough to lie and cover one hand, and he was in a mess. His mother had had him during the night, torn away the umbilical cord and a great piece of him with it, and then thrown him out of her box onto the concrete underneath. He was just about breathing when the keeper found him. When I saw him he was eight months old; a very trusting little animal. Unfortunately as they get older they often lose that trust and become very unreliable. It's a crime to keep them as pets. Nobody ought to have exotic pets except for a very good reason indeed . . . like an animal too badly injured ever to survive in the wild.'

Fitz looked at the monkey, which was stuffing its mouth with banana.

'He should have a good mixed diet; they're very like humans in their needs. Which is for variety. Lisa, phone this number and ask if Mr Stannard can put you on to someone who will have a note of the monkey lady's address and phone number. There's only one chance for this fellow and that's to see if she would take him in and nurse him; and I'd hope keep him. But it costs money to keep them; so she may not be able to take it on.'

'Never a dull moment,' Tim said, wishing briefly that there were a few. He was hungry again, and he had to operate on a dog that had been brought in to surgery with a broken leg that needed setting. The dog, a young black and white collie, lay miserably in one corner of the hospital, tied by his lead to the radiator pipe. The leg lay at an unnatural angle beside his tail.

'How did it happen?' Tim asked, as they lifted the dog carefully to carry him into the surgery.

Tamsin shrugged.

Behind them the monkey suddenly began to chatter as if he were swearing at them.

'I think he wants more food,' Lisa said. 'But he already has a very upset tummy. So what do I do?'

'Try him with a bowl of arrowroot,' Tim said suddenly, remembering his Aunt Dora who swore by the stuff which had been spooned into him as a child when he had an upset inside. She used it on her dogs and Uncle Sam had only with difficulty prevented her from trying it on a sick horse, in a bran mash.

'Although that's probably the silly suggestion of the day,' Tim said, as Tamsin began to anaesthetise the dog.

'I doubt if we can do much more harm,' Tamsin said. 'You know, we've never had a monkey here before. I don't know anything about them.'

'Very few people do,' Tim said. 'It's the last animal I'd recommend keeping. It must be a tremendous amount of work; diet; keeping them clean, and that's not easy. I once saw a baby monkey at the Zoo in nappies; which had to be changed and washed as often as a baby's and if they came into the keeper's house for nursing they all wore nappies as they don't house train. They don't need to, do they?'

He was waiting for the anaesthetic to take effect,

talking to try and forget how hungry he was, wondering why anyone ever thought it romantic to work with animals. There were times when it felt like slavery.

'Why don't they need to?'

Tamsin was almost as tired as Tim.

'They live in trees; so that if they just perform where they sit it falls well away from them, and as they move around a lot they don't get areas completely fouled up. After all, the jungles are big places, and people don't normally go walking underneath trees there as we do in civilised countries. Even so you're at risk from birds here which have the same habits for the same reasons.'

'What about foxes?' Tamsin asked.

Tim was now operating and the question was left unanswered as he drew the leg into the correct position and began to work on the injuries. The leg needed almost re-building and for some time there was no sound to be heard in the room but the tick of the clock and their own breathing and that of the dog.

'That's it,' Tim said, taking off his operating gown and putting it in the bin for washing. 'Let's get him back in the hospital. Better put him in a cage this time. I hope the monkey's gone. If I know Fitz he'll be driving through the night to get it to its new home. If she can take it.'

'The monkey's gone,' Lisa said, a few minutes later. 'Fitz said he's sorry but till he gets back you're solo; the hero on his own. Meg's in bed with flu and he's off to the wilds of Wales. The monkey lady will take our problem patient and the owners don't want him back; in fact they don't want him back so badly they didn't even grumble when Fitz suggested they made a handsome donation of £5 a week for his keep till he's better, and then gave a lump sum by way of thanks. They're pretty well off as there are about six grown up sons and they all live at home and all work.'

'How do sailors live at home?' Tim asked.

'He comes and goes, silly.'

'I hope nothing does happen tonight,' Tim said. 'I feel as if I've been up for about eighty hours; come to think of it, I almost have. Where are my dogs?'

'Mark came over and took them out for you; he thought it time they had a walk and as I seem to have left home permanently according to him and he has to get his own meals he might as well have some company and a change of occupation. Poor Mark. He shouldn't have married a veterinary nurse who lived on the premises.'

'It will be different when the baby comes,' Tamsin said.

'I doubt it; I hope to come back; you can baby sit for me,' Lisa said.

'When you've all done with planning my family life perhaps you'd care to join me in a small collation,' Mark said, putting on the voice of one of their posher clients, who always used words that nobody but her understood and who often came in to surgery with a very elegant Borzoi bitch, who managed to have the oddest things wrong with her. Usually things that embarrassed her owner to talk about, like the day she had been extremely sick every hour on the hour. When Tim went out to see her, as she was too sick to bring in the car, he had examined the mess she produced and suggested it might be wiser to feed her dog food instead of cowdung which she had obviously eaten in great quantity.

'The carpets are all gorgeous, and very pale cream,' Tim had said when he came back. 'You should have seen Mrs Lah di Dah cleaning up, looking as if she needed a gas mask, and without a clue how to do a decent job of work. She said she'd get someone in to clean all the carpets, or she might just sell them and replace with new ones.'

'If Lady Jane's going to live on cowdung her owner needs a pretty steep bank balance or she'll be changing carpets every month,' Lisa had said. It was obvious when Tim glanced at their faces that they were all remembering the incident.

The door was flung open suddenly and banged against the wall as Dana and Zia leaped through.

'I left them tied up,' Mark said, looking at them as if he couldn't believe his eyes.

Tim unfastened the ends of the bitten through leads from the dogs' collars and held them up.

'Mark proposes; dogs disposes,' he said. 'That's two leads you owe me; my best leads, given me by grateful clients for my wonderful work on their dogs, gold plated, ten pounds each.'

'Come off it,' Mark said. 'They were ancient relics from Aunt Dora by the look of it; chewed by generations of puppies.' He laughed. 'Oh well, no harm done except to two leads. I've made soup and sandwiches since it seemed that nobody was going to eat tonight. A little bird told me Meg has flu.'

'What little bird?' Lisa said, taking two sandwiches and pouring coffee from the flasks which Mark had brought across with him. She collapsed into a chair. 'Thank heaven for small mercies and large husbands.'

'I was more concerned with what you were doing to our baby, working a thirty six hour day, so it's pure selfishness,' Mark said. 'Actually it was Meg herself. She rang through to say I was to tell Lisa she was feeling much better and not to bother to call in before bedtime, as she's made herself a cup of hot consomme from a tin, and is going to sleep for thirty hours at least.'

'Lucky old Meg,' Tim said. 'I remember sleep. It's rather a nice feeling; a soft warm bed, a ticking clock, darkness, and nothing happens until the alarm tells you it's half past eight and it's Sunday and your day off. Cor, if only life were like that.'

'Eat, drink and be thankful you are fit to do it,' Mark said, passing the plate to Tim who took five sandwiches, and sat on the window seat, holding his cup of coffee carefully, warming his hands on it. He must be tired, he felt so cold. Surely to goodness he wasn't also getting flu? He shivered. He couldn't have flu. He couldn't possibly have flu; not tonight with Meg ill and Fitz on his way to Wales with a sick monkey.

The phone rang.

'Sara, for you,' Tamsin said a moment later, holding out the phone.

Tim swallowed a sandwich that he felt ought to taste wonderful but that tasted of nothing. He didn't know if he wanted to eat or not. He sipped his coffee which also tasted odd. Maybe he had monkey poisoning. He couldn't possibly have flu.

'Hi,' he said into the mouthpiece.

'I rang the Foal Bank,' Sara said. 'They had a mare come in today that lost her foal. She wouldn't take our baby at first but they've put the skin of the dead foal on ours, and they think that the mare will accept him by morning. She's beginning to take an interest, and not kick out every time the foal tries to feed. They've got a round the clock watch on him; it sounds a wonderful place, Tim.'

Tim had a sudden overwhelming desire for bed.

'Good,' he said, wondering if it was his voice or not. His brain seemed to have stopped working properly. 'Let me know how he goes on, but not till morning, please.'

Sara laughed.

'Be seeing you,' she said.

'Are you OK, Tim?' Lisa asked.

'I hope so,' Tim said. 'Better give me some first aid

71

remedies fast; aspirin or something, or maybe I ought to try a syringe full of equine flu vaccine.'

'Can you cope?' Lisa asked. 'You look rotten.'

'That's a big help,' Tim said. 'I have to cope, don't I? I only hope that Fitz doesn't succumb before Meg is better; look all right won't it if we're all laid low. Better see if Mr Stanton can cover for us if I do have to pack up.'

Tamsin dialled a number.

She made a face after speaking into the phone.

'Joe's got flu and Mr Stanton's out at a calving; so we just pray the phone doesn't ring and produce an emergency,' Lisa said.

'It heard you,' Mark said, as the bell pealed into the room and Dana barked, as she was standing right beside it and it startled her.

'Quiet, nut,' Lisa yawned, and looked at the clock. Tamsin was making notes on the pad and Tim drank the liquid she had just given him hastily and thought he had better pray for strength. 'Like having a midnight feast,' Lisa said sleepily. 'I'm calling it a day. Sorry folks. I don't seem to have the energy I had before I started the baby.'

'You won't have a baby if you don't come home and get some sleep,' Mark said.

'Trouble?' Tim asked as Tamsin put the phone down and looked at the pad.

'Jersey calf that refuses to be born; out at Hangman's Leap. The farm's called Golden Acres . . . it's not a long drive but whatever else you can do, you aren't fit to drive. I'll just ring through to Mum so she doesn't worry herself sick all night and I'll take you there. Finish your coffee.'

Tim drank his coffee, wishing he felt better. That Jersey herd was worth a small fortune. They had sold their last bull for thousands of pounds; if this was a

72

good little bull calf he could be worth a great deal of money; and even a heifer calf would be worth good money when she was grown. The farm took most of the awards at the County shows; it was a magnificent place. They rarely needed a vet as they could do most things themselves.

If they had called him it was really tricky.

And he had a temperature and was developing a sore throat and felt slightly sick and very shivery.

And there was nobody else to cope.

6

The farm was on the hills, and Tim, leaning back in the passenger seat of Tamsin's little car, began to feel distinctly sick. The headlights lit an endless winding lane of hedges, with very few trees. Insects swam into the headlights and vanished. An owl flew beside the car, pacing it for almost a mile. He tried to concentrate on the world outside himself but was aware that unless they arrived soon, and he could take something to make himself feel better, he was going to be working under greater difficulties than he had ever known.

'It's cold,' he said, and Tamsin accelerated, knowing he must have a temperature. The little car was too hot for her.

The farm was large and the yard was floodlit. There was electricity in the stalls and Tim was relieved to see that he would at least not be outside in the pouring rain that had now begun in a steady downfall.

He could hear the cow bellowing. .

'It would have to be our best cow; she won every prize there was last year and this calf, if it's born alive, will be worth something, not only for milk, but for breeding. It will make the record books if I've chosen the bull well. His sons and daughters are all magnificent.'

Tim thought of Meg, safely in her bed. Lucky Meg. If only he were in his; if only he were home with his mother fussing over him, bringing him hot water bottles and hot drinks, keeping the room warm. If only he didn't need to think, to work, to use all the wits he had and more. It was so easy for something unexpected to happen.

He would have to warn the farmer.

'I tried to get someone else to come out to you,' he said, the words coming with difficulty from a throat that was rapidly becoming raw. 'Mr Fitzgerald is on his way to Wales with a very sick monkey in need of care, and no one else can give it to him. There's an expert there; and Meg's got flu, and so I am afraid, have I.'

John Silver was a sensible man. He looked at Tim for a moment, and then nodded his head.

'Fair enough,' he said. 'First of all indoors with you; hot tea and aspirin; and my sheepskin coat when we come outside. You can make all the examinations and tell me exactly what to do; you aren't fit for that. I appreciate you coming out under the circumstances. I'll do exactly as you tell me, and if things go wrong, then no one's to blame but bad luck and the cow choosing to calve tonight of all nights. And doing it wrong.'

It was a relief to have decisions taken out of his hands, and to let someone else lead him into the warm, and sit him by the fire, while Netta Silver glanced at him anxiously and went to put the kettle back on the fire, and then went to her medicine cabinet.

'This will help,' she said, taking a small packet out of a cardbox box and mixing the powder inside it with hot water. 'It takes a few minutes to act. Polly's not going to hurt if she's left a few minutes longer. She's trying to produce a calf that's lying wrong, but we sent for you quick as John knew; he always does.' She smiled at her husband and poured tea for Tamsin and handed her a plate of home-made scones dripping in farm butter. 'You won't feel up to eating, Mr Yorke.'

Tim sat and sipped the hot liquid. It was bitter, and

he found it difficult to swallow. Tamsin had put her cup on the table and was checking through his veterinary bag. The ropes for bringing the calf were in a polythene bag, lying on the table. He tried to check through the procedure. He wouldn't be able to examine the cow wearing a sheepskin coat; that was for sure, but if John Silver could do all the work himself . . . he'd been farming long enough. He never did deliver an awkwardly placed calf, though. He always sent for Fitz.

John Silver. Why did it sound familiar and why couldn't he think about the calf. His mind hopped about like a grasshopper. A tabby cat was lying on the hearth rug, purring as four kittens fed from her. Their paws kneaded against their mother's fur, and she turned her head to lick at the smallest, which was lying nearest to her mouth.

'It must be nice to be a kitten by the fire,' Tim said, trying to shake off the feeling of lethargy that was making concentration so difficult. He didn't want to get up. He wanted to stay here, feeling safe and warm and sleepy and to sleep and sleep and sleep. 'Why does the name John Silver remind me of something else?' he asked, the thought niggling.

'Treasure Island,' Netta said, laughing, as she poured herself a cup of tea. 'Long John Silver. Everybody is reminded of him and half of them don't know why. John's father had a funny sense of humour.'

Didn't do me much good at school,' the farmer said. 'I changed my name to Jack; that didn't remind people so much. I'm used to it now. Not many farmers are commemorated in a book, even if it was written a long time before I was born!'

'If we don't go out now, I won't make it,' Tim said. His legs ached and his head ached and his arms ached. He began to feel that even his clothes were aching.

John Silver picked up his sheepskin jacket, and followed Tim outside, while Tamsin brought the bag and ropes.

'Will he be all right? He looks dreadful,' Netta Silver said.

'I think he'll cope,' Tamsin said. 'We rang Mr Stanton but they're in the same boat; his assistant has flu and he's out at a calving. I could leave a message for him to come on here, or maybe we could ring him later; or if it's a long job perhaps Fitz will be back.'

'We'd have to cope if we were snowed in and on our own,' Netta said. Tamsin smiled, and went out into the wet and windy dark. Half a gale was blowing and the trees round the farm were creaking noisily.

She went into the byre, where Tim was standing against the cow, examining her. John Silver held her still, or as still as was possible, as every now and then she flicked out her hind leg, or struggled against the restraining men.

'The calf's lying with both front legs curled under it, instead of being stretched out,' Tim said. 'It won't be born till we can get those straight. Also it's a very big calf; bull calf, I'd guess.'

'I wanted a little bull; want one of my own breeding, as a lot of farmers round here would like to use him.'

'It's alive, anyway.'

Tim wasn't at all sure whether Netta's medicine or the needs of his own work were making him feel better, but he was going to bring this calf himself. Blow having flu. There wasn't time to think about his own feelings. He was only aware of the job in hand; of the straw covered floor at his feet, of the breathing of the cow, and her bellowings as she struggled to free herself of a calf that couldn't be born; of the farmer's soft voice soothing, talking gently to Polly, who occasionally seemed to stop and listen to him, and of his own hands, feeling deep inside the cow, feeling the legs, easing them gently, wishing he could see, could introduce some instrument into her with a screen to the outside that would show a television picture, instead of having to work by instinct and by experience and by feel alone.

This is what it was like to be blind.

Feel, very gently. A pull here, a push there, easing the legs, aware of sweat dripping off his face and Tamsin wiping it for him; aware that she was watching every movement he made and that the farmer also was watching him, aware that if he wasn't very careful he could end up with a dead mother and a dead baby.

This was what his job was about, but there was nothing to be done but do the job; people thought it romantic; it wasn't. It was a job, and he was covered in muck; there would be more muck before the end.

He withdrew his arm. He had one leg in the right position and the second leg still needed correction. It wasn't easy to reach and he was so tired.

The wind was increasing steadily, a nightmare sound outside.

There was a rending crash as somewhere near a tree uprooted itself in the wind and all the lights went out.

John Silver said something forceful under his breath and Tim leaned against the wall wondering if his legs had turned to jelly.

'Torch somewhere and handlamps; and if Tamsin can cope I'll start the generator. That tree must be down across the power line; it's all we needed,' the farmer said. He moved away and fumbled in the dark, but before he could bring light his wife was at the door, a torch in one hand and two big handlamps in her other hand, dangling by straps.

'Good girl,' John Silver said, and grinned at his wife who grinned back at him, knowing how relieved he was to see her, and aware that even being a grandmother did not age her in his eyes.

Tim was back with the cow, reaching in, feeling the second leg. He didn't want to use the ropes unless he were forced to do so; it wasn't easy and he wasn't feeling well enough to think clearly.

'All right?' Tamsin whispered.

'Just about. I'll manage, I think,' Tim said. 'Can't hurry it.'

You couldn't hurry anything with animals, Tim thought, as he moved his hand again and felt the hoof. He could never quite get over the astonishment of delving into the cow or horse or sheep or even a dog and feeling the living baby inside.

Netta Silver was standing where her husband had stood, talking softly to the cow. The cowman had just come in and stood with her, ready to help if he were needed.

'Worried about her when I went home, but I thought it would be tomorrow,' he said. 'I couldn't sleep with the wind and all.'

Sleep? What was that, Tim thought.

'What time is it?' he asked.

Tamsin glanced at her watch.

'Nearly two o'clock,' she said.

Two o'clock and all's far from well. Tim wondered what the old nightwatchmen would have made of a situation like this, and then as the leg eased into position and the calf lay correctly, he wondered absurdly if it hadn't been most annoying to hear the watchmen yelling in the night, on the hour every hour. Two o'clock and all's well. What if it weren't?

Tamsin wiped his face again, and he straightened up. He must be delirious.

There was a sudden bellow from the cow, deafening them all and then a tremendous heave, and the calf began to emerge. Within minutes it was almost out, and as the cow thrust again to expel it, it came out with so much force that it cannoned into Tim, who was off balance, and went down in the straw with the live and very damp calf on top of him. He lay there, the breath knocked out of him and thought how absurd he must look.

Netta Silver and the cowman lifted the calf and at once began to wipe the birth membranes away from its head. It twitched an ear and made a small whimper and took a deep breath and then another. Tim, sitting in the straw, covered in straw and muck, was grinning idiotically, and Polly, who had had two calves before, was already turning her head to see this baby she had produced, and struggling to reach him.

'A super little bull,' John Silver said exultantly a moment later, coming back into the stall just after the generator had throbbed into life and restored the lights.

'We can cope now,' he said, as Tim stood up and leaned against the wall. The cowman turned his head.

'You look rough, Mr Yorke,' he said, concern in his voice.

'Flu,' Tim said. 'All we need just now and it's early in the year for an epidemic.'

'There's a lot of it about,' the cowman said, and Tim caught Tamsin's eye and felt an absurd desire to laugh.

'She's pretty exhausted,' he said instead, making a mental list of procedures necessary after birth had been completed. He was about to go to her when Polly suddenly stood foursquare, and bellowed loudly again, and everyone watched in astonishment as a second calf fell to the ground.

'Twins,' the farmer said. 'Who'd have thought it? She didn't look that big.'

'She's a big cow,' the cowman said. 'She's also

enough milk for quads as a rule so we don't need to worry about this pair. Little heifer this one is. I've a nice clean stall ready for them; got it ready before I left. I was sure we'd need it in a day or two.' He went out of the door.

'Jim always does know,' John Silver said. 'I don't know what I'll do without him; he ought to have retired years ago but I can't get a stockman to replace him; he's nearly eighty. He's a wizard with animals; no sentiment, but plenty of kindness and commonsense.'

Tim was too busy examining the cow to make sure everything was well with her to have noticed Jim go quietly out of the stall. The man moved softly all the time, gentle movements that never startled any animal. He seemed to know without telling just how they felt and to have an instinct all his own to help them accept him. Many animals were too frightened when they were ill to be sensible and often associated the human trying to help them with the pain, and bit or kicked. Jim knew just how not to be attacked when he was trying to help.

He returned a few moments later with a warm drink for the cow. She was busy with both her babies, looking as if she knew she had produced a double bonus for her owner. She had no time for the people about her.

'Come into the house and have a warm by the fire and another dose of medicine,' Netta Silver said. 'Then you can have a look at her when the men've cleaned them all up and got them tidy and check nothing's gone wrong. It's rough out here and you need to clean up as well; I've run you a hot bath and Tamsin has your clean clothes warming by the fire.'

Tim, lying in hot water, wished he was always so well cared for. It was bliss to relax and soak but he had to be careful he didn't fall asleep. He dried himself and dressed and went downstairs.

He looked at the clock. It was after four. He drank the bitter brew, making a face and took his cup of tea. It was too hot to drink and he put it down on the table.

It seemed only moments later that he was being shaken awake.

'It's almost seven o'clock, Mr Yorke,' Netta was saying. 'We let you sleep and Tamsin had a lie down on my spare bed so she's had a sleep too. Polly didn't seem to need your help and it was a pity to wake you. If you have a look at her before you go . . .'

Tim was feeling much worse and a chair wasn't the best of places to sleep in. He wasn't sure whether he ached from falling asleep in a sitting position or from flu. He borrowed the sheepskin coat gladly and went out to the yard, where milking had almost finished.

'She's over here,' John Silver said, leading the way across the yard. It was littered with large branches and smaller twigs from last night's storm, which had now blown itself out. Tim skirted the puddles and went into the byre, where Polly looked up at him, her face placid, and two honey coloured calves stood sucking busily from her. He patted her toffee coloured head, and looked into her deep brown eyes.

'You're a clever girl,' he said.

'She's fine,' he announced a few minutes later.

'You'd best get home and get to bed,' the farmer said, as Tim and Tamsin climbed into the little car.

'If only I could,' Tim said, as they drove out of the yard. 'I bet Fitz isn't back yet; and Meg will be in bed for a few days, I should imagine.'

'Your imagination seems off beam,' Tamsin said a few minutes later, as they walked into the surgery. Meg, wearing her white coat, was operating on a cat that lay on the table.

'Road accident. He has a fractured jaw,' she said. 'There's no peace for the wicked. Can't even have flu in comfort.'

'You can get back to bed, young lady,' Fitz's voice said from the doorway. 'I can take surgery; and Tim looks as if he's spent the night in a cow byre and been trampled on by a herd of wild ponies. You got flu as well?'

'Or something,' Tim said, collapsing suddenly into the chair by the door. His teeth were chattering so hard he thought they must be audible to the people waiting outside.

'Home to bed. I'll take the dogs for the day,' Lisa said. 'Sleep; you'll feel a lot better this evening.'

Tim nodded. It was too much effort to talk. He pulled himself together and walked slowly across the yard. Every step seemed an effort and it had never been so far. The dogs were in the office and he had heard them crying but hadn't even the energy to go and greet them.

He felt as if a stick insect could knock him over by jumping at him.

His bedroom was warm. Lisa had put the fan heater on, and there was a hot water bottle in his bed. He shed his clothes on to the floor, pulled on his pyjamas and dropped on to the pillows, lying looking at a ceiling that seemed to be closing in on him.

He had never felt so ill in his life. He was sure he had pneumonia and probably brucellosis and tick fever as well. Or maybe catscratch fever or distemper. You couldn't feel like this just with flu. Perhaps he had parvovirus.

Lisa, creeping into the room an hour later, found him sound asleep. She drew the curtains to shut out the day, put a jug of lemonade and a glass of the surgery's own special anti-everything medicine on the bedside table and crept out.

She did not need to creep. Tim slept on, even when a dog came in that barked outside his window; even when the telephone rang constantly, even when Fitz, singlehanded, with too many calls and too many emergencies, raced from surgery to car, slamming the car doors, revving the engine, roaring out of the yard; even when Dana and Zia, sure they had been abandoned for ever, sat in Lisa's little sitting room and yodelled to the sky, begging Tim to come and take them home again and make life right for them.

They hated changes, and Tim was theirs for ever.

They couldn't understand it when he neglected them for so long.

They longed for him to come and fetch them.

Lisa, walking into the room later that evening, took one look at Tim and sent for the doctor. It had obviously done him no good at all to spend a night with a calving cow when he was so ill he ought to be in bed.

7

Tim had never been so ill in his life. It was almost a week before he even felt like eating. He knew that Tamsin and Fitz and Lisa were in and out of the room; that the doctor came and went; that somehow he managed to get himself up and washed and then crawl miserably back to his bed again, that somewhere his dogs were crying for him, but that was all he knew.

He woke on the sixth morning feeling distinctly hungry and weak as a new born kitten. His legs seemed to have a mind of their own and not to take him where he wanted to go. But the sun was shining and life seemed definitely something to be cherished. For the past few days he had not much cared about anything at all.

'Good,' Tamsin said, appearing in the doorway, seeing him sitting up in bed, instead of lying flat staring at the wall or the ceiling. 'Are you hungry?'

'Ravenous,' Tim said, suddenly realising that he had not eaten for days.

He attacked the food with pleasure; boiled egg and toast and marmalade; a cup of tea that tasted like nectar instead of tasting evil. 'I'll be up and about in no time at all.'

'I'm not so sure of that,' Tamsin said, removing the tray. 'Up, yes, but you're going to find you don't feel nearly as good up as you do in bed. One or two people have been very ill with this bug, and you're one of the two.'

'Who was the other?' Tim asked.

'Lisa. She's a bit better today but she's had a rough time. It's a good job Janet wants to work here, as Fitz has persuaded Lisa to work part time from now on and to give up completely except for visiting us, when Janet starts.'

Tamsin was right, Tim soon discovered. He dressed later that day and went downstairs, where the two dogs came in from next door and greeted him with such enthusiasm he was almost knocked over. Dana, who was rarely over affectionate, crawled on to his lap and lay in his arms, licking his face now and then to show her pleasure, while Zia leaned against his knee making odd little companionable grunts of pleasure. Tim was content to stretch his feet out to the fire which Tamsin had lit for him and do nothing very much. He switched on the radio and found himself listening to a concert of light music which suited his mood. Outside the blue sky added to his feeling of total relaxation.

He was well enough to heat the soup that Tamsin had left him and also to tackle the pasty and salad that was on the kitchen shelf, out of the way of the dogs.

'How's the invalid?' Fitz asked, calling in that evening.

'Felt fine till about half an hour ago,' Tim said. 'I feel ready for bed and it's only half past six.'

'You won't feel like a day's work for another week at least,' Fitz said. 'Luckily I've been able to get one of my retired colleagues to come for two weeks. Meg's not completely better either and I don't want two invalids on my hands for the rest of the season. I've sent her home to her mother to be fattened up for Christmas. How about you? What about a week with your Aunt Dora?'

'I think she'd finish me off and my mother couldn't take the two dogs for a week and I don't much want to leave them behind me,' Tim said. 'I think I'd rather be here and potter about. I can go up and see Sara, and maybe by the end of the week have a short ride on Hawk. Don't feel like driving that far either. It's idiotic.'

'Not so idiotic,' Fitz said, as he went to the door. 'There aren't many people who spend their first night with flu and a raging temperature in a cow byre. Those Jersey twins are both thriving; nice sturdy little calves. I went up to see them yesterday. John Silver sent you this by way of thanks.'

He put two jars of honey on the table.

'Their honey is the best I've ever come across. Mrs Silver grows special flowers in her gardens for her bees. She's a real bee lady; knows more about them than I do. She thought lots of good pure honey would give you energy and she sent this to add to it.' He put a basket down on the table and went out.

Intrigued, Tim took the cloth off the top of the basket and found himself looking at home baked scones and bread; a cut and come again cake, as Aunt Dora had called them, being the kind you could put away for a week and bring out for visitors without it going stale; a dozen large brown eggs, and a pound of farm butter, as well as a jar of cream.

He put everything safely away, and let the dogs into the garden.

'The dogs have been in the isolation kennels, as nothing else is there,' Tamsin said, a few minutes later, having seen them from the office window. 'I'll feed them and put them there for the night.'

'Leave them here,' Tim said. 'I can cope. If I come down in my dressing gown, and have a biscuit in my hand they'll go out, empty and come straight in. I taught that to them some time ago; it's very necessary when I've an emergency call to make. No time for messing about.'

It took very little time to feed them. He weighed the food, added water, added their seaweed powder, which Aunt Dora insisted on sending him as she was sure it did more good than anything any vet could offer, and watched them eat. They both ate as if they would never be fed again, and then began the routine that somehow had started when Dana insisted that all her meals had to end with a slice of brown bread which she adored.

Food finished, they went into the garden again, and came in for three small dog biscuits each. Off they trotted to the kitchen, where Dana barked in front of the bread bin. Tim cut a thick slice of brown bread, halved it and gave it to each dog.

It was now time for Zia to insist on her special treat so that she led the way to the refrigerator and butted the door hopefully with her nose. By now both dogs were drooling, and as Tim opened the refrigerator door, they sat, eyes on every movement, watching him take out the cheese, open the packet, cut off two pieces each about two inches square and return the cheese to the shelf again. They edged towards him, both in a sitting position, shuffling along the floor.

Dana barked and Zia whimpered, and Tim handed each her own piece of cheese.

At last the ritual was over, and the two bitches walked soberly to the sitting room, each to her bed. Zia stretched out, her paws dangling over the edge of the bed, and Dana curled up, nose buried in her thick black and white tail. She looked more and more collie like as she grew up.

A glowing fire; a meal of farmhouse food; two dogs lying in their beds, and the radio playing music. Tim wanted nothing else. He stretched his legs to the blaze, sitting in his deep armchair, and thought that life was perfect.

From this distance even delivering calves had a slightly romantic glow about it; he had a good job, and he loved his cottage, which was the first home he had ever had of his own. He had freedom for a week; freedom to do as he chose; to get up when he chose; to eat without the demands of his job; to go to bed early and know he wouldn't have to be up at dawn and out in the car and then in a cow byre.

He glanced out of the window as a Land Rover drew up. A tall man with a dense shock of thick white hair climbed down from it. He was dressed in breeches and boots and the oldest jacket Tim had ever seen. He came up the path and knocked at the door.

Tim let him in.

'I've just been over to see young Sara; that new mare of yours was a big mistake, wasn't she? She's in a pretty poor way. I'm Tom Gennet, by the way; known young Fitz for ever. We were both at college together but he was in his first year when I was in my last. Used to take him with me when we went out to see cases on the farms, and I was demonstrating, as his dad and mine were great friends.'

Tim, who thought Fitz definitely elderly, was amused to hear him referred to as being young. He invited the newcomer in.

'Make the most of your rest, young man,' Tom Gennet said, looking at the scones on the table. 'Those look good.'

Tim laughed and fetched a plate and a knife and watched the older man tuck in as if he hadn't fed, and then realised that he almost certainly hadn't.

'Have you eaten today?' Tim asked.

'Not so's you'd notice. It's been one of those days.

Twin calves at 3 a.m. Fitz was called out in a hurry to a possible case of swine fever, Thank heaven it wasn't. So I took surgery. Just to make my life perfect a dog came in that had gashed its leg on glass and cut an artery. Luckily the owner didn't panic but took off his tie and put it round the leg above the wound, with a wadded hankie to make a pressure pad, and we saved its life. I followed up with the oddest case I've ever had . . . a pony that got her leg caught in a ram's curled horn while he was lying down in the same field.'

'What on earth did you do?' Tim asked. He was cutting up a pasty that Lisa had made him, adding baked beans and frying potatoes, as he talked. Tom Gennet had stretched out in Tim's chair, and Zia had her head on his lap, her eyes adoring him.

'Nice bitch. Going to breed from her?'

'I don't know,' Tim said. It had just struck him that Tim and Tom together sounded like drum beats. Tim, tim, tom, tim, tim, tom. He must still be a bit light-headed.

'What did you do about the pony?' he asked, fetching knife and fork from the kitchen drawer.

'We had to cut the poor ram's horn off; you never saw anything stuck so tight. Goodness knows how she managed it.'

'They do the oddest things,' Tim said. 'I had one horse that broke its neck by catching its harness on a nail as it reared in fright. Some fool had put it away with the bridle still on.'

'I had a dog that jumped a spiked gate and got caught by the collar; that broke its neck too,' Tom said. 'People don't realise how easy it is for an animal to get into trouble, or that animals can't think. We have to for them.'

He began to eat, and Tim banked up the fire, and sat down. The two dogs started to play, rolling over one another, biting at one another's fur, growling in mock anger, a play growl that Tim ignored.

'Some people would think that dangerous,' Tom said, laughing at the dogs. 'It's extraordinary how little people understand about animals they live with.'

'People don't understand people,' Tim said with some feeling. 'So it's not really surprising they don't understand dogs.'

Tom laughed, and looked longingly at the fruit cake.

'Aunt Dora sends me one of these every month,' Tim said, as he cut a slice, 'which is very noble of her, considering the postage costs.'

'I had an odd encounter this morning,' Tom said. 'The trouble was that the man I was visiting was blind and nobody warned me; and he thought I was Fitz which didn't help matters at all. So there we were having the weirdest conversation as he was insistent I knew what was wrong with the dog, wasn't doing my job properly by forgetting, and he was so angry he wouldn't listen to me.'

'Makes me remember one of our more awful occasions when I was at school,' Tim said. 'In a way it was my fault, but it wasn't really. We had a neighbour who lived alone and I suppose being lonely spent a lot of the time looking out of the window at us all. One day my mother was going to the Sales in January and going off early, and I was to go off to school after my sister had left. Mother told me to make sure I pulled back the curtains before I went.'

He broke off, grinning, and cut a second slice of cake.

'Best cake I've tasted in years,' Tom said. 'I live alone since my wife died and I never cook; eat in pubs or off my lap. Go on.'

'I forgot,' Tim laughed. 'When I got home Mum was

furious, as when she got home the phone rang and the old lady said very angrily "Where have *you* been?" "To the sales." "Oh," and she rang off. Mum then had a visit from next door. The old lady seeing the house all dark and no one about had rung the police and said we were all lying there dead from a gas leak!'

Tom laughed.

'What did the police do?'

'Apparently crawled round the house sniffing under the doors, couldn't smell gas, assured her there was no one in and likely to be an innocent explanation and went, but she wasn't convinced and tried to get several of the neighbours to break in. She spent most of the day ringing up and of course no one was there to answer. It was months before she spoke to Mum again, but it had all taken place in her own head!'

'You get that all the time,' Tom said. He stretched back and threw a small piece of bread to Dana. Zia got it first and Dana came back to look hopefully at Tom.

'Don't allow titbits,' Tim said, with a smile to take the edge off the rebuke.

'Very wise. Nor do I.' Tom offered Dana a tiny crust and came to sit down on the other side of the fire.

'Make the most of your week off,' he added. 'You'll never have it so good again.'

'I'm realising that,' Tim said. 'The real trouble is I haven't the energy to do half the things I want to. I was going to ride Hawk.'

'That's another thing you aren't going to do,' Tom said. 'Goodness knows how he's done it, but he managed to pull a tendon, apparently doing nothing whatever except try and look over the hedge at a mare in season down the road. She's been whinnying her head off to him and he's been calling love songs back to her. It's bedlam; both of them are surrounded by very high very thick and very prickly hedges, or we'd have them having assignations in the road.'

'It's as well they don't stay in season,' Tim said. 'Anyway, Hawk's a gelding.'

'He doesn't seem aware of the fact though,' Tom said. 'And that's what matters. It wasn't done long ago was it, and I believe he's been used as a stallion twice as well.'

'I suppose Sara hasn't any news of that foal,' Tim said, pouring coffee.

'I suppose Sara has,' a voice said behind him, and he jumped.

'Sorry, I did knock but nobody heard, not even the dogs.' By now Sara was fielding off both of them. 'I can't stop; too much to do, but Mum called on me and she's horse sitting. The mare's picking up; she's lived on bran mash but now I'm beginning to build her up a little with a more normal diet. She isn't quite as ribby as she was.'

'Sara's had a lot of work to do on her; she was very nervy and scared of people and tried to bite,' Tom said.

'She trusts me now. I sat in the stable and read a book, whenever I could, to get her used to having me around; now she doesn't leap out of her skin every time I go near, or rush to the back of her box and look agonised, which is a relief.'

'What about the foal?' Tim asked.

'That's why I've come. It's being fostered by a mare that has lost two foals in succession through sheer bad luck. The first was born just before a clap of thunder and she reared and came down on it and killed it. The second was born in a field just as a flash flood started; they got to the mare, but the baby drowned. They live in an area where the floods can come very fast and frighteningly and they hadn't been there long enough to realise how fast it was. They have the mare in a safe field now. They'd like to buy the foal from us. His mother won't be able to feed him ever so it could be a very good idea.'

'It would,' Tim said, glad that for once they were able to agree. He had been afraid Sara would be sentimental about the foal; he had few illusions about the way women got too attached to animals. Four of his main problems were geese that had been bought for Christmas and nobody could ever kill. One of them made his life a misery by chasing him whenever he came near, which wasn't helpful when it needed treatment. Tim had undignified memories of racing for his life across the yard pursued by an infuriated gander with a badly damaged wing who wasn't going to allow anyone he didn't know near him. They had managed in the end, but it had been tricky for half an hour or more.

'They've offered more than I paid for the mare,' Sara said.

Tim grinned at her. He had caught the defensive note in her voice.

'OK. I won't complain again,' he said.

The phone rang.

'Tim, is Tom Gennet there? A dog's in surgery; it's been run over.' It was Lisa's voice.

'Road accident, in surgery,' Tim said, and Tom was out of the door almost before he'd finished.

'I must go too,' Sara said. 'I've Hawk's leg to put cold poultices on, and the mare needs another feed; she's having very little and very often; and I can't leave Mum there for ever.'

Tim closed the door behind her, and went back to his chair.

He had never been really ill before in his life and he wished he felt better. Somehow everything seemed an effort. He was glad he hadn't to get up and see to Hawk's leg, or deal with the road accident. He was glad

94

he had a large fire and two dogs and no need to work.

He couldn't understand why he felt left out.

Everyone was busy but him; and he was useless. If there was another road accident, he wasn't fit to cope.

Wearily, he stood up to let the dogs out, and watched them as they went into the garden. They came back fast and dropped by the fire again, and Tim switched on the television set, to distract himself. He had never felt so miserable in his life and he didn't know why.

Within minutes he was sound asleep while the figures on the screen played out their roles, and shot one another and screamed and danced and one programme followed another.

He woke at midnight to find the screen blank and both dogs in their beds.

He let them out for the last time, and then went up to bed himself, wondering if he would ever feel well again or if he was doomed to crawl around feeling half alive for the rest of his days.

8

A week later, lying on his back in cow muck with another hefty young bull calf on top of him, which had come out rather faster than anyone had expected after hours of trouble, Tim found himself wishing he were back by the fire.

He grinned to himself as he drove back to the surgery. Nobody ever had what they wanted. A week ago he had been miserable because he wasn't working and this morning he was wishing himself back with time to spare again.

Tom Gennet had gone.

Meg was back again, and Janet had just started in the practice, with Lisa now working only in the mornings, showing the newcomer what was involved.

Janet loved the work but was very shy and found it hard to answer the phone or talk to the clients. That surprised Tim who had thought her very confident in club, but she had been coming to club for three years, ever since she was thirteen and was on familiar ground there. Here everything was new and she had more responsibility and was afraid of making mistakes.

'I'd forgotten how much there is to learn,' Lisa said at coffee on Janet's fourth morning. 'You take it for granted when you know it all. I told Jan to prepare a compress for a cat with an abscess and forgot she didn't know how or where anything was kept. Or even how to handle a very cross Siamese with an abscess on his tummy.'

'How did he get it?' Janet asked. She was destined never to know as everyone was so busy. She wanted to learn, but there was so much to learn and people forgot to tell her things from the beginning and expected her to know without being told. Fitz had a dreadful habit of racing in and telling her to get him so and so and she couldn't even remember the name of what he wanted, let alone find it.

Tim had sent her to find some of the calcium compound he injected into calving cows with calcium deficiency and when she had forgotten the right name had said 'the stuff for eclampsia, of course,' and not even realised poor Janet was nearly in tears and he had been abrupt because he was extremely worried. Calcium deficiency had to be dealt with fast as it made animals very ill indeed, and where an owner could rush a bitch into surgery, nobody could rush a sick cow there; he had to find the stuff and get out there fast. He had used the last in his bag the day before and not had time to tell Lisa to replace it.

Time seemed to be disappearing again. The days flew by. He operated on a pony with a rupture; he went out to three sheep that had been mauled by a dog. The farmer had shot the dog, but hadn't killed it, and it had run off and everyone was hunting for it. It had to be put to sleep when they found it and he hated doing so. It had been very badly hurt, and had bitten him.

He operated on a cat with a fishhook stuck inside its mouth; it had tried to eat a newly caught fish with a length of broken fishing line in it. The owner hadn't bothered to remove the hook before bringing the fish home. The cat had stolen the fish. It was a difficult operation as fishhooks have barbs and the cat was in agony. The pain was as bad when he woke up from the operation and he had cried so piteously everyone had been upset.

He stitched up a cut leg; and had a dog come with a split pad which was going to be long and difficult as no way could a dog be kept from walking. He had a puppy that had a stoppage in its intestine. Nobody quite knew why it happened but it sometimes did and if not treated fast the puppy died. The operation wasn't always successful and a lot depended on nursing afterwards; the puppy had come in almost too late and Tim had operated with the fear that it was too late and he would be blamed when it died. It was a relief to see it running around a few days later, apparently none of the worse for its experience.

There was a bad scare when a farmer thought he had a case of foot and mouth disease which meant slaughtering all the herd. Tim had driven out there with a feeling of total panic and been very relieved to find that it was nothing so serious at all. The cow had a cough from eating some dusty hay that hadn't been intended for her; she had come home from the field by herself because someone left the gate open, and the rest of the herd followed her. They had gone into the yard but she had gone through the yard to one of the barns, and found the hay that had been dumped there to be thrown out as it wasn't fit for feeding.

He injected sheep against foot rot.

He injected dogs against distemper and hard pad and leptospirosis which came from food contaminated by rats. He injected them against parvovirus, which was less of a problem temporarily in his area, though it might come back.

He injected cats against feline enteritis.

He injected pigs and he tested cattle to make sure they didn't have TB. He injected horses against tetanus. He began to dream of syringes; filling them and injecting animals, and then heard of a friend of his who had injected a cow against contagious abortion.

She had panicked, and twisted on him; his friend was in hospital having had the syringe turned into his arm and emptied by the frantic cow. Noboby quite knew what an injection of contagious abortion would do to a human. It stopped the cow losing her calf. Everyone laughed when they heard what had happened to poor old Simon but it wasn't really funny.

There was an epidemic of gastro enteritis and every dog he saw had been sick, and was still being sick.

'I suppose there are other vets in this practice,' he said irritably to Lisa one morning. 'I seem to be single handed and never see either Fitz or Meg.'

'They say the same about you. Meg's gone off to another foaling; Fitz is testing a herd of cattle this morning. You have four cats to neuter, a bitch to spay, and there's a goat that needs a Caesarian in the outhouse.'

Tim dropped wearily into bed that night wondering if he would be allowed to sleep.

He hadn't been asleep more than ten minutes when he heard a wail from downstairs.

Dana had been very sick.

He cleared up and was about to go back to bed when she was sick again and he realised that he was about to have another disturbed night. Zia raced round the room unhappily every time Dana was sick. Tim laid the bitch on a pile of newspapers and made up the fire and watched her. He couldn't understand why she was ill as she wasn't behaving normally for a dog with gastroenteritis.

He thought back to supper time.

He had, for the first time that he could remember, added two eggs to both dogs' feed. Zia had been brought up to have raw eggs occasionally but Dana had never had them before, and he now suspected she was allergic to eggs.

He gave her some kaolin mixture which made her sick again.

There was nothing much he could do. If it was an allergy she was better to get rid of everything bothering her. He put Zia in the kitchen and shut the door and Zia cried and scratched frenziedly to come in.

By four in the morning Dana was asleep, and Zia had gone to her bed where she lay miserably awake almost as if wondering if she would be ill, or if Dana would make those horrible noises again.

Tim made himself a cup of cocoa, and at four thirty dropped on his bed fully dressed. He woke at six, listening.

No sound.

He went downstairs and both bitches hurled themselves at him as if he had been gone for ever and a day. Dana ran into the kitchen and stood by the refrigerator door, behaving as if nothing had been the matter with her.

Tim gave her a spoonful of her usual food, and gave Zia a biscuit. If Dana kept that down he would know it was only an allergy and not a bug, and he could go about the day's business with an easier mind. He wished he had had more sleep. Somehow things always went wrong when he'd had a bad night.

By the time he had eaten his own breakfast Dana was playing with Zia. The night troubles might never have happened. No more eggs for Dana, and nothing with egg in it either. He would have to warn the girls not to give her cake.

He went across to the office to take surgery.

Janet was in tears and Lisa was angry. Sheila looked at him with a stony expression on her face. Tamsin was walking about flicking dust off the bottles, behaving

100

as if each were a personal enemy.

'What have I done?' Tim asked, puzzled.

'Nothing. The RSPCA inspector is here with a dog. I hope you feel strong.'

'I was up all night,' Tim said. 'Dana was sick every ten minutes; I gave her eggs for the first time and she's allergic to them.'

'The best of British luck then,' Sheila said. 'I've seen a lot in my time, but . . .'

Tim looked at her, and went into the surgery. He stood for a long time, looking down at the dog that lay on the table and then, without even glancing at the Inspector, got out his syringe, and injected the animal in the leg. It had no energy left to move; they watched it drift off to endless sleep. They stood without speaking for some minutes.

The RSPCA Inspector looked at Tim.

'I needed witnesses,' he said. 'I'm going to prosecute.'

Tim looked down at the dog. It was a big dog, covered in appalling sores and matted fur. It was so thin that it was only bones with skin and tangled fur. The eyes had run and were septic; the paws were bleeding, and it was so gaunt Tim didn't know even what breed it had been. The fur was so filthy he couldn't tell its colour.

'Kept in a shed behind a dump, chained all its life; never cleaned out and I don't think it's been fed for weeks. It was very hard not to kill the owner,' the man said.

Fitz, coming in, took one look, fetched his camera and took four photographs. He said nothing either. It wasn't the first time, it wouldn't be the last and they never got used to it. The photographs would be needed for the court case. Fitz always took them himself when a bad case came in.

Tim went to the office.

'I'm going to write I HATE PEOPLE all over the waiting room walls,' Lisa said. She began to cry, and Tamsin decided that she would be better at home.

Fitz nodded.

'Waiting room's full, I'm afraid,' he said. 'I'll see half the people in the little extra room. Better clear that up quickly; and see the table is well sterilised before you put the next one on it; heaven knows what the poor brute had wrong beside just that. Probably everything under the sun.'

Tim hated the jobs that followed, but at last he was ready for the next patient, and wondered wearily what would come through the door.

What did come in was Janet, with half a grin on her face, which was still tear stained, and with two small boys with very solemn faces.

'It's our gerbil,' they said. 'He's getting very fat and mummy says he has a swollen tummy and there's something wrong with him.'

'How long have you had him?' Tim asked, as he opened the box.

'Four days. We got him from Johnny at school. I swopped him for four marbles.'

Tim had forgotten about schoolboy swops. It was such a relief after the last case he found it hard not to laugh, and he ruffled the two small boys' hair. He lifted out the gerbil and then he did laugh.

'It's not funny,' one of the small boys said, and he realised they were twins, very alike in face though dressed differently.

'It's not a he, it's a she,' Tim said. 'And she's going to have babies; either tonight or tomorrow; you'll have little gerbils too. Would mummy like that?'

'She doesn't like him anyway,' one of the boys said. 'Look, mister, can we swop him?'

102

'What for?' Tim asked.

'That big poodle of yours. We haven't got a dog.'

'How old are you?' Tim said.

'We're six.'

'She's a bit big for a six year old,' Tim said. 'I'll tell you what. You take some of these leaflets about pets home; there are all sorts. See if your Mum would let you have one of those; a tortoise might be a bit easier, or a goldfish. And we can keep your gerbil here till she's had her babies and look after her properly as they would your mum if she went into hospital to have you.'

'She's going in to have another baby soon,' one of the boys said. 'If she has a girl we want to swap it for an . . .' he paused and took a deep breath, thinking hard, 'a baby elephant, then we could ride it to school.'

Tim swallowed and Tamsin, coming back, led the two boys outside and gave them all the leaflets she could find.

Tim stood at the table shaking with laughter, unable to let it out. Tamsin, returning gave a whoop, unable to help herself.

'I wish surgery wasn't so full,' she said at last, wiping tears from her eyes. 'Tim, supposing that gerbil needs a Caesarian and has to have the babies cut out of her, could you do it?'

Tim looked down at the tiny animal.

'Let's hope she does it properly,' he said. 'I can't bear anything else today. I've never operated on a gerbil in my life.'

It was a relief to have a simple case next time. A cat with ear canker. He gave the owner some drops, and some advice and marked down the treatment on its card. It was a big sandy cat with a twisted ear.

'Great fighter in his time,' the old man said. 'He's nearly fifteen now.'

'He's a very healthy cat,' Tim said truthfully as the

animal purred and rubbed its head against his sleeve. It was well looked after and the ear trouble would clear up in a couple of days.

He was thankful when surgery ended at last and Janet made coffee.

'Honestly,' he said, as he picked over the biscuits and took one covered in bright pink icing that made Meg shudder, as she liked hers very plain, 'I feel as if I'm in never never land today; don't know which way up I am.'

Tamsin went into the hospital and came back three minutes later, unable to tell them why she was laughing so much.

At last she was able to get the words out.

'Do you know anyone that would like sixteen gerbils?' she asked.

9

Tim had just finished his afternoon calls when the phone rang at the farm he was visiting. The call was for him. He put down the receiver and stood, frowning.

'Trouble?' Sam Hunter asked, leading the way outside. Tim had been testing his herd of pedigree Friesians, with Janet writing down the procedure for him and which cows had been done. Janet enjoyed her days on the farms. It made a change from answering the telephone and Fitz liked her to take her turn as she wanted to be an animal nurse, and was working hard for her exams.

Tim nodded.

'Sorry, we'll have to do without that tea you promised us. Apologise to Mary, won't you?'

Sam and Mary were rapidly becoming friends, as Tim was often called in for one animal or another on the farm, which was a very large one, with cattle, a flock of Anglo-Nubian goats, a variety of cats of all colours that specialised in frequent litters of attractive kittens, and five Shire mares, as well as the farm hunters and the children's ponies.

'What kind of trouble?' Janet asked.

Tim looked at her.

'Hero. Somebody's knifed him and almost cut off his paw and Jock thinks it's the end for him; he's bleeding badly. Tamsin's put on a pressure pad and they are taking turns to keep pressure on; but he lost a lot of blood, and Fitz is away at the Beast Sale; the usual vet's got flu, and Meg was called out to a calving. So we hurry. No talking, OK?'

Janet nodded. She had learned that when Tim was thinking about his job he was almost unaware of other people; he tended to speak to them as if they weren't quite there, his mind on whatever animal was on the table waiting for examination or surgery. Now he was concentrating on driving fast, well and safely, pushing the Land Rover to the limit to get back in time.

Janet watched the hedges flash by, saw a weasel run across the road, saw a pheasant strutting in a field; watched cattle grazing, and caught a glimpse of a heron, fishing in a stream. Tim reached out and switched on the radio and music flooded the air. Within twenty minutes of leaving the farm Tim was drawing up in the yard, grabbing his bag and running into the surgery.

He looked down at the dog. It was their local police dog, a big handsome fellow, with a lovely temperament, able to switch on fury when told, and to frighten the life out of the local villains. Jock Macrae stood beside his dog, his mouth grim, his eyes desperately anxious.

'OK Jock, out,' Tim said. 'I'll do what I can. No promises. He's in a very bad way.'

'Aye, I know that,' Jock said, and followed Janet out. Janet took him into the office, and went to make coffee. Jock was one of their favourite clients and they all loved Hero who never made any sort of fuss when he needed treatment and he needed it often, for one injury or another. He led a very active life in an area where, Tim had decided, the favourite pastime was breaking milk bottles. Hero was always cutting his paws.

Tamsin had everything ready, and Tim was able to

start work at once. Shock; infection; control the bleeding; reduce the amount of pain. He removed the pressure pad and looked at the knife wound. The paw was almost cut in half.

'Can you?' Tamsin asked.

'I'm going to try,' Tim said.

It needed concentration to repair the paw; to match every part of it to the severed part; the dog was severely shocked; he had lost a great deal of blood and there was going to be a risk for some days. Tim was only half aware of his thoughts; he was concentrating intently on the job in hand, and Tamsin, from long practice, handed him what he needed, said nothing and was never in the way.

Fitz, walking into the office a few minutes later, heard Jock's story, looked in, and Tamsin shook her head at him. He closed the door quietly and started on the people waiting to see Tim who should have been taking that night's surgery.

Jock sat on in the office, his cold coffee untasted beside him, his thoughts next door with his dog. Hero had been part of his life, and a very major part of his life for six years. A wise dog, well trained, able to think for himself, hearing the slightest rustle at night, aware of danger, his ruff prickling, the fur on end, the deep soft growl that immediately alerted Jock to trouble brewing. They were often called out on county cases, well away from their own regular beat as there were never enough dogs.

Jock's mind went back to nighttime tracks, searching for people who were lost. The old man who had fallen and broken his ankle and might have died if Hero hadn't found him in time; the child who wandered away from a picnic and was cut off by mist from his family; the people who went out on a good day and climbed too high and were trapped; Saturdays at football matches; political demonstrations, always with Hero to give him the kind of aid that no man could give another man, because no man had ears so sharp, or such fast reactions.

He looked up as Tim came into the room.

'I think his chances are fifty fifty,' he said. 'I'd like him here over night; we'll sit up with him in turns and if there's any sign of collapse from shock one of us will be there at once; if you have to bring him in you might shorten his chances. He knows us, and he'll be warm, and it's better not to move him, or jolt him in the van anyway.'

'Can I ring later?' Jock asked.

'Whenever you like, as someone will be up anyway. I'm sorry, Jock, but I can't promise anything. You do know that.' Tim looked at the man anxiously.

'I won't blame you, whatever happens,' Jock said. 'The joker who did it is under lock and key and he'll get what's coming to him; it's one of the risks of the job.' He went out, and Tim went into the hospital room where he and Tamsin had carried Hero. The big dog lay quietly, still anaesthetised. They wouldn't know anything for at least twelve hours. And even then he might be crippled, or the injury might infect and there was always a major danger from that.

'I'll stay with him; go and eat and see to your dogs,' Tamsin said. 'None of us has had time for them since five o'clock, and they haven't been fed.'

Zia and Dana were in the little isolation room, which was empty of patients. They had been put there when Jock came in as everyone was far too busy to worry about the dogs. They greeted Tim as if he had been away for several centuries and romped in front of him across the yard and into the cottage. Mrs Fitz was standing at the gate talking to her gardener, who was a major part of her life, as she adored her flowers, and was always trying new varieties of rose and clematis. Tim nodded to her, but she was too deep in conversation to notice him, and as always was elegantly dressed, even though she had been working in the flower beds.

Somehow Mrs Fitz always seemed to manage to make the man work overtime very happily as he found he could try out all kinds of new ideas with her enthusiasm to back him. He grinned at Tim, who found it hard to grin back, as he was very worried about Hero.

The dogs were waiting for him to open the door. Both were hungry and raced in and straight to the kitchen where Dana barked at the feed bin.

'OK, greedy,' Tim said, as he picked up the big metal bowls both dogs sat watching him, little pools of saliva dribbling from their mouths to fall at their feet in a pool. Zia, the more impatient of the two when it came to food, stood and put her paws on the draining board and was told off for her behaviour. Meekly, she sat again, but inched her way hopefully towards Tim who was so tired that he found himself unable to concentrate and forgot what he was doing, and gave Zia double quantity and almost none to Dana and had to start again.

At last both bowls were ready and both dogs had barked for their food, as he was teaching them to speak on command. Dana squeaked with excitement, unable to get her noise out, but Zia had developed a full throated bark and barked eagerly and noisily.

The evening was cold and there were the ashes of yesterday's fire. Tim couldn't be bothered to clean them out. He was tired and he was hungry. He plugged in the electric fire, and put a frozen pie in the oven to cook. He could heat potato crisps and open a tin of peas. It wasn't an ideal meal but he didn't feel like cooking. He put a plate to warm and rang through to Tamsin.

'How is he?'

There was only one 'he' that night.

'Holding his own; breathing normal; not coming out of the anaesthetic yet, but he was under for a long time. Do you know how long that op took, Tim?'

'Yes. A year,' Tim said, and rang off.

It had probably taken a couple of hours, he thought; he didn't really care so long as it worked and the dog survived. He couldn't bear it if Hero died after all that effort to save his life. Jock would have to start again with a young dog and that would mean that he was also penalised, as no young dog could ever do the same excellent job as the experienced wise old fellow.

A tongue licked Tim's hand and he jumped.

He had forgotten the feeding ritual. He fetched three biscuits each, cut the thick slice of brown bread and gave each dog half and then cut the cube of cheese, the dogs chasing from their bowls to the pantry, back to the bread bin and then to the refrigerator, knowing each stage perfectly and anticipating it, and nudging Tim impatiently because he was so slow.

He decided he was still affected slightly by the after effects of flu. He felt drained of all energy. Then he remembered that they had only had a cup of coffee and two biscuits for lunch as they had intended knocking off early and having one of Mary's enormous high teas. No wonder he felt whacked.

It was good to sit down and stretch his feet to the fire, even if it were only an electric fire; to sit and eat quietly, without interruption. He couldn't be bothered with the television set; it was too noisy, too fast paced and often too irritating. He found a cassette of his favourite music, the Peer Gynt suite that contained 'In The Hall of the Mountain King', and put it on, letting the sound wash over him. He kept it very soft and it soothed the day's worries, so that presently, his plate set aside, he fell asleep in his chair, with one dog's head on each foot.

He woke at midnight and his first thought was for Hero. He called the dogs and put them in their beds. They went at once, thinking he was going up to bed, and watched surprised as he took his anorak and went out into the dark. He wondered at their surprise; and then wondered if they associated the ringing phone with his nighttime departures. The phone hadn't rung to call him this time.

Tamsin had the big chair from the office in the little warm room and was reading. A large female cat lay in one cage, an animal Tim hadn't seen before.

'I think she'll need a Caesarian,' Tamsin said. 'Fitz kept her in for observation as he says her kittens are huge. She's not started yet, but she might at any time, so it's just as well we're keeping an all night watch.'

'All we need is for her to start and Hero to collapse,' Tim said, feeling that too many problems came together and pushed them to their limits. Nobody would feel very lively in the morning. 'Get off to bed; are you staying with Lisa?'

'Yes. She's made me up the spare room bed; it's routine now and the baby won't make much difference; I don't exactly make a lot of work for her, as I always strip the bed off and wash the sheets for her. Mother's a bit of a worry at the moment; her heart's getting dickier and I don't like being out too much at night.'

Tim nodded. Tamsin worried about both her parents, but she couldn't give up her job as she helped to keep them both. Her father had been unable to work for some years and his pension was very small.

He picked up the book Tamsin had left. He had never heard of the author, but it looked like a good thriller and that was what he needed to keep him awake. He bent over Hero, who was beginning to move, whimpering softly as the anaesthetic wore off. He stroked the dog's head gently. He'd miss his master; but there was nothing Tim could do about that. As yet the dog was still only partly conscious and everything appeared to be normal. The paw was bandaged and they had done all they could for that.

The doorbell rang and Tim jumped, startled.

All he needed was another emergency.

He opened the door.

Jock was standing on the doorstep.

'I couldn't sleep and the sergeant's given me three days off, as I was cut too. I got a kick in the ribs; got a cracked rib, I've just discovered; the hospital sent me home, thank goodness.'

'When?' Tim asked.

'About an hour ago. I did go to bed and got up again. Then I thought I might as well be here as at home; I can sleep when I know he's OK. You can go off to bed if you like; tell me what to watch for and I'll watch. He's my dog . . . and I can't leave him if he's dying. I want to be with him.'

'I'll make coffee,' Tim said. 'Just watch for twitching or sudden panting; I'm only next door.'

He came back ten minutes later to find Jock kneeling by his dog, who was awake and looking into his master's face. His tail beat a faint tattoo on the floor, and he licked Tim's hand when he bent over.

'I think we can give him about an eighty to twenty chance,' Tim said. 'He's as strong as any dog can be, and he's coming round normally and that tail's a sign that he isn't anywhere near at death's door. Only trouble is he might be lame for life.'

'I don't care about that; I can keep him as a pet then, and either get a second dog or go off the dog section,' Jock said. 'I'll have that coffee now; haven't had the heart to eat or drink all day.'

'Then you'll eat,' Tim said. 'Watch him and I'll go and make you some sandwiches. Ring me on that if there's the least sign of trouble. You know your dog better than I do; and you know what's normal and what isn't.'

Tim ran across the yard and let himself in. He was used to making food in a hurry and within minutes was back again with meat and tomato sandwiches and a large slice of Aunt Dora's cut and come again cake for both of them.

They ate and drank with rising spirits as Hero woke and began to wag his tail again.

'I'll get my mother to make you the biggest cut and come again cake you've ever seen,' Jock said jubilantly, an hour later, as they looked down at Hero, who was sleeping quietly, with no sign whatever of any major trouble. 'One of the advantages of living alone is being able to do things like this; if I'd a wife . . .'

Tim nodded. There were advantages to not being married when your job took you out at night. You couldn't disturb anyone going out or coming back and there was nobody to worry about if you were late, or delayed.

He left Jock at about two o'clock and went off to bed, knowing the dog was in the best possible hands, as Jock was a devoted owner. Tamsin, ringing through a little later, knew she need not come down. Jock told her he would go home and sleep if the dog was still behaving normally in the morning and then maybe he could take him home.

By morning Tim was delighted with his patient, and everybody, meeting in the hospital, anxious to see how Hero had fared during the night, was rewarded by a wagging tail and by the sight of the dog trying to stand on three legs and walking shakily to the door to ask to be let out. Jock put him on his lead and took him into the garden and brought him back a few minutes later, grinning all over his face.

'He even tried to chase your cat, the villain,' he said. 'He's not so clever though and he fell on his side and lay there as if asking me what I'd done to make him lose the use of his legs. He's not doing badly, is he?'

'He's doing fine,' Fitz said. 'We'll take care of him all day; and I see no reason why you shouldn't pick him up this evening. Go and get some sleep. You've been in the wars too, they tell me.'

'News does get around,' Jock said, as he went outside to his van. The police van was a familiar part of the scene to Tim; they often passed one another and flashed their lights in greeting, Jock on his way to an incident and Tim on his way to a case. Jock without Hero was unthinkable.

He let his own dogs out, gave them their morning biscuits and went across to the office with them. They settled at once in the familiar corner, both glad to be with him again and back to their normal routine. If he had an easy day he would be able to take them out that evening and walk them off their paws; he needed a walk. He longed for nothing to do; it was his free evening. Tomorrow was dog club and he might also make that, if . . .

He went back into the hospital to look at Hero, who was half sitting, lapping a bowl of milky food.

'He seemed hungry,' Tamsin said. 'Light meal. 'OK?'

'Fine,' Tim said and was startled by one of the noisiest purrs he had ever heard. He turned round, to discover the she-cat licking a newborn kitten to clean it, purring at the top of her voice as she did so.

'Who needed a Caesarian?' he asked.

Tamsin came across.

'She looks fine. Better put a cloth across the front of

the cage; we don't want her disturbed by people. She'll yell if anything goes wrong but by that demonstration everything's going very right. What heaven!'

It was a quiet day for a change; with few people in surgery and nothing that was at all serious. Tim bandaged a cut paw, removed a thorn, gave somebody a tin of flea spray, and gave another dog owner worm pills for the routine worming that all good dog owners did automatically every three months as the dogs were always getting reinfected from other animals whose owners weren't so careful. He clipped a poodle's claws, and gave two puppies their first injections, both owners having been well aware they had to keep the pups in the car till surgery was over to avoid infection from other dogs. Sometimes an older dog might be sickening for something that wouldn't make him ill but would make a young puppy very ill.

'I'm celebrating with a cordon bleu meal tonight,' Tim said at teatime, exultant that for once the day had gone well. The she-cat had five healthy kittens and was nursing them, purring so loudly they could hear her in the office.

The noise amazed Hero, who got up twice to try and look at her, but she was in a high cage, and he couldn't see. He sat, his head on one side, his ears pricked, as cats were not part of his home life. Cats were to chase if Jock didn't stop him; for all his training he was still a dog and he knew very well when he was on duty and off duty. On duty he wouldn't dream of giving chase to a cat, but off duty no cat was allowed to invade his garden.

Tim looked at the injured paw when Tamsin removed the dressing. There was no sign of infection; it would take time to heal; but it looked as if it was going to heal cleanly. He had injected antibiotics to make quite sure. Hero sat watching everything that was done, and then began to drum his tail frenziedly on the ground as he heard Jock's voice in the passage.

'No need to ask about my dog,' Jock said.

Hero was standing, asking to go home.

'Go on, you ungrateful animal,' Tim said, laughing and stood watching as man and dog went off. They all watched Hero climb into the van, into his familiar place and settle down, after a brief bark at Dana who was standing with her paws on the window ledge watching him go.

'Makes it all worthwhile,' Tim said.

'That's what it's all about, my boy,' Fitz said, coming to stand beside him and watch the police van go. 'A day to chalk up in your memory and look back on when everything's black. A day to tell your grandchildren about.'

Tim, who wasn't married and hadn't thought about children, found the idea of remote grandchildren even more unlikely and grinned, but he whistled as he walked to his cottage and whistled as he played with his dogs, and discovered that the after effects of flu had completely vanished, removed by the sense of total achievement he had felt as he watched Hero climb into the van, only a day after he had thought he would have a dead dog on his hands.

He looked at the calendar and solemnly ringed the day with a red circle. A day to remember.

10

Tim looked about him with satisfaction as he drew up in Sara's yard. Everything was as he liked to see it; the cobbles clean, the stables tidy, the wise heads looking at him over the half doors. He rubbed Hawk's neck and whispered to him and was rewarded by a gentle push against his cheek with the velvety muzzle, and then went on to look at the little rescued mare.

He hadn't seen her for three weeks. She had flesh on her, and her coat was beginning to shine; she was a pretty animal, nicely made, with the high carried tail that showed she had Arab blood in her. He looked her over approvingly. Sara had not made such a big mistake after all.

'Coffee,' Sara asked from behind him. He turned and the mare reached out and nipped his shoulder.

'That's one thing you have to watch out for. She's unhappy when she's groomed too,' Sara said. 'Hates her legs being touched in any way at all. I'll have to get her steady before the blacksmith comes. This new man is impatient. Not like old Joe who had all the time in the world for horses. Now it's all time and motion study and earning as much as you can. Hallo and goodbye with the money, before you have time to turn round. The horses don't like it.'

Tim hadn't met the new blacksmith. Joe was well over eighty and even then had had to be talked into retiring.

'I'll die if I retire,' he said mournfully, and was delighted when one of the local farmers offered him a retired Shire horse to keep him company and to look after. He walked Monarch out daily and the villagers were used to the sight of the tiny old man and the grey muzzled black Shire, walking slowly round the streets and lanes together. Nobody could remember how old Monarch was. Well over thirty, the farmer thought. Neither of them would last a great while longer and they'd be missed when they were gone. As it was, come high day or holiday, weekend or weekday, rain or hail or shine, Joe and Monarch took their daily constitutional.

The old horse had hollows over his eyes, but those eyes were still wise and he had seen everything in his time. He had been paraded and had won awards. He had drawn the big drays and he had competed in the Agricultural fairs. He had once been harnessed with three of his mates and they had pitted their strength against a traction engine. Neither side won.

Tim watched for the pair of them, and grinned when he saw them. It always made his day. Joe had more knowledge in his little finger than most modern horsemen had in their heads, but it was hard to prise it out of him.

'Penny for them,' Sara said, wondering why Tim had gone into a daydream. It wasn't like him at all, but his attack of flu seemed to have slowed him down.

'I was just thinking about old Joe and Monarch,' Tim said, following Sara into the little sitting room where a bright fire glowed in the grate, the wood logs spitting. A cat with kittens was curled on a chair and she stretched herself as he came in. One of the kittens tumbled off the chair. Tim picked it up, looking down at the minute transparent claws and newly opened eyes that stared at him hazily. He tucked it on to the chair and sat down.

'No more mares, or foals, or horses, or ponies, or anything that costs money to keep,' he said, as Sara brought in the two steaming coffee mugs.

'No more,' Sara promised. 'We did make £100 on the foal; they were delighted with it and the foal bank did a marvellous job.'

'They always do,' Tim said. 'I was talking to Fitz about them. He can't speak highly enough. I must go down and look at the place sometime.'

'We did,' Sara said.

'For as long as it took to settle the foal; I want to look about; spend a whole day there and find out how they operate. It could be useful to know. If we're going to breed in future we may well want to use them again.'

'The little West girl is looking for a pony,' Sara said. 'They asked me to buy one for them, on commission; that doesn't go against your principals, does it?'

'So long as you earn money and don't pay it out,' Tim said. 'Thought I saw a new head in the end stable; what are you up to?'

'That's a livery mare. Her owners have been sent to Canada for six months, for the husband's job. Full livery, for eight months; they are leaving in three weeks time, and wanted her settled in before they went; and won't pick her up till they have been back a month and settled themselves.'

'And they pay when they come back, I suppose,' Tim said.

'No. They paid the whole lot in advance, in case anything went wrong with the transaction of sending money monthly from Canada. I signed an agreement saying I'd refund anything if she died meanwhile and that the only way I am liable if she does die is if it's by my own carelessness; if she gets flu and we can't save her, then that's their bad luck, I'm afraid; but if I ride her out and break her neck, then I am liable.'

'And fully insured, I hope,' Tim said. 'I also hope you priced it right. You need some reward for all the work you'll have to put in. Don't take too many livery horses; or you'll do a bad job, not a good one. Any sign of anyone coming to help yet?'

'I've a girl coming under the Government scheme; so that won't be too expensive. She wants to learn stable management and make her life with horses. We'll see how she shapes; mucking out on a beastly icy morning and grooming and feeding, instead of just riding and having someone else do the hard work cures all the starry eyed ones; we need those who can knuckle down and get a stable clean in as short a time as possible and turn out a horse as if ready for a show every day; I'm sick of seeing muddy animals with dirty eyes and flies round their eyes because nobody ever bothers to clean them.'

'That makes two of us,' Tim said. 'This won't get me to High Hills. I've been treating a cow with mastitis. I want to see how she's doing.'

He walked outside and over to Hawk and gave the horse a carrot. Sara was riding him daily to keep him fit as was necessary. Tim had a momentary vision of entering for eventing, or hunting, but knew there would never be time. He wanted to compete in dog shows; he wanted to teach Zia to track properly. Aunt Dora wanted Zia to have a litter when she was two; Fitz wanted him to take a greater share in the practice with a view to taking it over one day; everybody seemed to want something from him.

The cow had recovered, and he walked outside to look down on the valley. He loved High Hills, and the view from the farm gate. Everyone was busy and he was there only briefly. Behind him buckets clattered and voices called; a cow mooed and somewhere a cock crowed suddenly exultantly, and absurdly at the wrong time. Bantam cock by the sound, Tim thought.

He climbed into the Land Rover and Zia nuzzled his neck. Both dogs had been lying quietly, waiting for him. They were growing up and growing wise and were far less trouble. Pups were so full of life and lack of knowledge and were not aware of danger. Zia was more cautious than Dana, who was apt to rush at a farm animal and retreat in horror when it showed that it hated her. She expected all the world to love her, both humans and beasts and was always offended when they didn't.

He drove down the lane.

It was a bright day, the verges brilliant with flowers, the birds singing. Two magpies flaunted themselves briefly on a gatetop and flew off. There were sheep on the fields alongside the road, and large lambs among them. A hare jinked out of the hedge, and down the road in front of him and through the opposite hedge. He hadn't seen a hare for a long time.

He braked the car to watch and was aware of shouting.

He got out and walked to the end of the road, carrying both leads, the dogs behind him, at heel. He looked over the gate into a field. He put the dogs down by the hedge, tying their leads to the gate and fastening them. Couldn't be too careful.

Two girls were riding a Shetland pony, barebacked, galloping round the field, one hanging on to his mane, the other with her hands round her companion's waist. They were flailing him with a short riding whip, and Tim, looking at the pony's wild eyes, knew that in a moment there would be an accident.

The girls saw him, yelled whoa and the trembling pony braked and both shot on to the ground. They picked themselves up and walked across to Tim.

'Meg and Marie: and what do you think you're doing?' Tim asked.

'Riding our new pony,' Meg said. 'Isn't he lovely?'

Tim looked at the pony and swallowed. His hooves were overgrown and badly needed trimming and when walking he hobbled painfully. His chest was rising and falling in great heaves as he struggled to draw in air. He had been over ridden by two girls far too heavy for him. He was lathered in sweat and he had been whipped and was terrified. Tim walked towards him, and he galloped off to the end of the field and stood, watching, wary, not wanting to be caught and ridden like that again.

Tim took Meg's whip.

He slashed it through the air.

'Run,' he said.

'Do what?'

'Run, or I'll hit you.' He was going to show them how it felt to be made to do more than you were able. He might get into trouble but he found he didn't care. He was angrier than he had been for a long time.

'Run,' he said, and slashed the whip close to Meg's face. She stared at him, suddenly frightened by his grim expression and then began to run, her sister beside her. Tim chased them round the field until both were crying and then stopped them.

'How do you feel?' he asked.

He hadn't much need to ask. They were heaving great gasps to get in air; they were dishevelled and trembling, and leaned against the gate for support.

'I'll tell my mum,' Meg said. 'He's our pony.'

'I'll tell the RSPCA,' Tim said. 'You'll get prosecuted; look at him, with no flesh on him, with lice in his coat which you've probably got all over you, with a mane and tail nobody has ever brushed; with hooves that must be agony to walk on and when was he last shod? How's he fed?'

'On grass. That's what horses eat,' Marie said,

looking up at Tim from sly eyes.

'I'm going to see your mother. Come on. He's going to be left alone till his hooves are right, and he's going to be groomed; and he needs a stable. I wouldn't be surprised if he's sickening for something; flu or strangles,' Tim said, trying to make everything sound as bad as it could be. They needed to be taught a lesson, little horrors, both of them. They hadn't had a thought for the pony or its comfort or its feelings, but had raced it as if it were a machine.

Two hours later he drove a small horse trailer into Sara's yard and sat there, wondering just what Sara would say. Behind him was the Shetland pony. The family had parted with it for £10 rather than be prosecuted. It was in worse condition than Tim had realised; and it was sickening for something though he didn't know what and it would have to go in the isolation box at Sara's; and he had told Sara they were rescuing nothing more.

He looked at Zia. Dana crawled across the front seat and licked his face, not wanting to be left out.

'So what do I say?' he asked.

Neither dog could tell him. He patted them and grinned to himself.

Sara at that moment rode into the yard, and dismounted from Hawk.

'Since you never ride him, someone has to,' she said. She glanced at the trailer. 'I thought you said no more livery horses here? What's in there?'

Tim opened the back of the trailer and led the pony out.

'This is Prince,' he said. 'He has a pedigree to boast about, but you'd never guess it; he could be a marvellous pony one day.'

Sara's lips were twitching as she tried hard not to smile.

'I suppose you paid a fortune for him,' she said.

'I paid £10,' Tim said indignantly and then realised she had trapped him. The two of them stood against the trailer, unable to stop their laughter.

'Tim, Tim,' Sara said at last. 'You're as much of an idiot as I am for all your pretence to be hard hearted. The last thing we need is a Shetland pony that's sickening for something, is lousy, and look at the work he needs done on him.'

'It's my evening off,' Tim said.

'And the dogs haven't had any exercise and you're tired and you need a break, and you never get one and whose fault is that?' Sara said, getting slightly worked up and somewhat mixed up.

Tim put the dogs in the small paddock where they could run with the little grey donkey who loved them. They would get all the exercise they needed and it was impossible for either to get free. He led the pony into the isolation stall. He spoke softly to it and it relaxed, aware that this man meant no harm and that Tim wasn't going to get on the pony's back and ride him until he dropped with exhaustion. His hooves were hot and sore and his back ached and he was too hungry to eat.

Tim began to work on him. Delouse him; gently pull the tangled twigs out of mane and tail; gently groom him, drying him, cleaning him, making him feel better. The pony was too tired to resist; he stood, head hanging, feeling ill, with vague memories of better days when he had a clean stable and clean paddock and his mother's comfort against him. He was lonely and he was sick and he was miserable and he didn't much care if he lived or died.

Sara brought a warm bran mash out some time later, but the pony barely touched it.

'You've bought a pig in a poke,' she said. 'Suppose he

has flu? And infects all our other horses? Who does the nursing?'

Tim looked at a pony that was considerably cleaner and more comfortable than he had been . . . when? He glanced at his watch. He'd been working for three hours.

'Where are the dogs?' he asked.

'Indoors, lying in the fire, quite happy,' Sara said.

Tim had finished examining the pony.

'I think all the trouble is caused by laminitis,' he said. 'The poor beast's had every possible reason to get it; they let him drink when he was hot; they rode him hard on the lanes, with a hard surface to go bang bang against those overgrown hooves; it would be bad for a fit pony and no way is this fit. And that pasture is rich and heaven knows where he was kept before; they've had him two months. Look at the way he's standing; and he's got a temperature.'

The pony was standing in an odd position with his forehooves well out in front of him, as if he were trying to get his weight off them.

'With luck it's not longstanding; and this is the first time. We might just get him right,' Tim said.

Sara knew the drill and went for the mineral oil to dose him. She brought packs for his feet. Tim injected him.

'I'll get the blacksmith in tomorrow,' Sara said.

Tim glanced at the pony. The pony looked up at him. He was aware that these people were trying to help and wanted to show his gratitude. He began to tug thoughtfully at the haynet that Sara had fixed up close to him, where he could reach it but not get caught in it.

'He might do well yet,' Tim said.

It was dark outside. The dogs greeted him and returned to lie on the rug. Sara brought in a big pasty and cut slices off it, and handed Tim a dish of salad.

They ate in silence, both too tired to talk.

An owl called outside the window. Zia ran to the sill and looked out, her head on one side. The bird was perched on a fencepost at the edge of the yard and she watched it. Light from the window caught the edge of its head, and the rest of it was in shadow. Zia appeared puzzled, unable to see all the bird but only the disembodied head turning almost full circle, the light catching the eyes. Beyond the bird the shadowy branches of a tree moved, the boughs rustling in the wind. A train hooted, far away.

The dog walked back to the fire, stretched herself, nosed Dana thoughtfully and lay down.

Sara switched on the television set.

Barbara Woodhouse appeared, unexpectedly saying 'WALKIES', and both dogs barked and ran to the door.

'Oh, blow her,' Tim said, half laughing, half irritated. There would be no peace till they had been outside. He wondered if she knew what mayhem her programme sometimes caused.

He went outside and stood by the paddock watching the dogs run in the thin moonlight. The donkey stood beneath the tree, motionless, and they ignored her. Their needs were soon fulfilled and Tim put them in the Land Rover, and went to look at the pony. It lifted its head and whickered very softly in recognition. It was bedded on deep peat, which would be kind to its hot hooves. Sara brought in a bucket that had been standing in her kitchen. She never gave water straight from the tap. She had a large supply of buckets that were cleaned out thoroughly and re-filled and allowed to stand, away from the stable so that they didn't get full of dust and fouled by ammonia fumes from the pony's own waste water. That happened easily and then the ponies wouldn't drink; nor would horses. They knew what was clean and what was not, even if they did sometimes drink from puddles. Mud to them didn't matter; foulness did.

Tim closed the half door and got into the Land Rover.

Sara look at him.

'Who said no more horses?' she asked.

Tim grinned at her.

'This time I mean it,' he said. 'No more horses.'

He put the car into gear and drove into the lane, followed by Sara's laughter.

It was only a matter of time before they all heard of it down at the surgery and quoted his own words back at him. 'Sara has to learn you can't buy horses casually, just because you feel sorry for them.'

He had to learn too.

'No more horses,' he said very firmly to the dogs as he put them in their beds, as if it was their fault.

The dogs looked at him.

The words didn't bother them in the least. In just over a year they had learned a great deal about Tim and one of the things they had learned was that he was all bark and had very little bite at all. They settled down to sleep, knowing it didn't apply to them, whatever it was.

He lay in bed and watched the moon slip out of the sky, and said to himself just before sleep came,

'No more horses.'

Even as he said it, he knew that with Sara as partner and the stables there that he would be caught all over again when the next pony needed a good home; and he knew too that he couldn't take them all on. He and Sara would have to learn to leave well alone; but how did you learn?

He had no answer. He slept and dreamed that Meg and Marie were dancing round him, urging him to run with their whip, urging him on and on till he could scarcely breathe and his chest rose and fell and his heart hammered and the whip flailed and they jumped up and down like two little witches yelling 'No more horses; no more horses; no more horses.'

He woke drenched in sweat.

He laughed at his dream.

'All the same,' he thought as he drifted off again, 'it is a good idea. We'll both be stony broke the whole time, so no more horses.'

THE END

Life

The available facts reveal very little about Botticelli: his paintings tell us most about his life, indeed they reflect the ideas and mood of the late Florentine Quattrocento better than any other contemporary work. Neo-Platonism and the preaching of Savonarola interacted to create a period of spiritual upheaval in his native town during his life. We will first consider the chronological facts, and leave aside the question of his relationship with the society of his time until we examine the theory of art which was the true expression of his personality. He was drawn by temperament to the contemplation of Beauty as an ideal, and as a result his nature found little expression in action: anecdotes, therefore, sometimes a useful guide to the personality of an artist, are extremely rare.

The main events of Botticelli's life are quickly stated. He was born in 1445; this information appears in a tax-return belonging to his father, who was a tanner, Mariano di Vanno Filipepi. Sandro was sent to school in 1458, as we know from another tax-return, in which his father says: ' Sandro, my son, aged thirteen, is at his books and in poor health. ' A little later, according to Vasari, he began as an apprentice in the studio of Filippo Lippi (c. 1465), and remained there probably until 1467, the year in which Filippo established himself permanently in Spoleto. In the *Ricordanze* of Benedetto Dei we find that in 1470 Botticelli painted his work *Fortitude* (now in the Uffizi) for the Court of the Merchants (Mercatanzia). In 1474 he painted the *St Sebastian* (now in Berlin) for the church of Santa Maria Maggiore, and the same year left for Pisa, where he began a fresco, now lost, for the Cappella Incoronata of the cathedral.

From this time onwards nearly all the references to him concern the paintings: a standard painted for Giuliano de' Medici for an allegorical pageant set to music by Poliziano in 1475; in the year of the Pazzi plot, 1478, a series of portraits of the conspirators who were hanged near the

Palazzo Vecchio; and the *St Augustine* for the church of Ognissanti, in 1480.

In June 1481 Pope Sixtus IV summoned Botticelli, along with other principal painters from Umbria and Florence, to Rome to decorate the walls of the Sistine Chapel. He remained there until the spring, or possibly the autumn, of 1482. His father Mariano died in this year. There is also a record of a contract with the Florentine Signoria listing the names of Ghirlandaio, Perugino, Piero del Pollaiolo and Biagio d'Antonio Tucci, for the decoration of the Sala dei Gigli in Palazzo Vecchio. Only one of these frescoes was carried out: Ghirlandaio's *St Zenobius,* which is still extant. An altarpiece (now in Berlin) was painted in 1485 for the Bardi chapel in the church of Santo Spirito. The Uffizi *Annunciation* for the church of Cestello (now Santa Maria Maddalena dei Pazzi) dates from 1488-90, and in 1491 he was one of a panel of judges, with Baldovinetti, Ghirlandaio, Perugino and Lorenzo di Credi, at work on the commission for the façade of the cathedral of Santa Maria del Fiore.

Botticelli's brother Giovanni died in 1493. Giovanni was called *il Botticello* ('little cask'), from which it is generally assumed the painter's surname derived, though Vasari denies it. In 1496 he received a letter of introduction from Michelangelo in Rome to Lorenzo di Pier Franco dei Medici, in whose Villa at Castello he executed various decorations the following year. In 1499 we have the only reference which links his name with that of Savonarola; on 2 November his brother Simone Filipepi wrote in his journal: 'My brother Alessandro di Mariano Filipepi, one of the best painters we have in our city, was seated in my house by the fire at three o'clock one night. He told me he had spoken about Fra' Girolamo (Savonarola) with Doffo Spini in his workshop that day. Knowing that Doffo had acted as a principal during the interrogation of the friar, Sandro questioned him and asked him to tell the whole truth. He wished to know what sins they had found in Fra' Girolamo, which caused them to condemn him to that dreadful death. Doffo said: " Why did you condemn him? " He replied: " I did not condemn him, our leader was responsible,

Benozzo Federighi. If we had let him return to San Marco with his friends, the population would have pillaged our goods and torn us to pieces. Things had gone so far we had to put him to death to save our own lives. " The bluntness of this report and the single wary question put by Botticelli can leave little doubt as to his reformist sympathies. The anguished and prophetic style of the final paintings seems further to support this view.

Nearing the end of his life, in 1501, Botticelli painted the *Mystic Nativity* which is now in London. He planned, through his contacts with Annabella Gonzaga's agent in 1502, to complete the decoration of Isabella's Studiolo, begun by Mantegna. Botticelli's popularity as an artist had by this time declined. This commission, which he would gladly have accepted, had already been rejected by Perugino and Filippo Lippi. In 1504 he was a member of the commission set up to decide on the final location for Michelangelo's *David*. He died in 1510. His name was entered in the *Libro dei Morti* (book of the dead) of the city of Florence and that of the Physicians and Apothecaries' Guild, to which he had belonged since 1499. His remains were buried on 7 May in the cemetery of the church of Ognissanti.

To complete this brief account of Botticelli's life, it is worth turning to Vasari's *Lives,* that great panorama of Italian artistic civilization, for a judgment by a near-contemporary on Botticelli's status as a painter. The reference to Botticelli is perfunctory and inadequate; but this is not the place to attempt an assessment of Vasari's true qualities as a critic and as a biographer.

Vasari begins: ' In the time of the illustrious Lorenzo de' Medici the elder, which was truly an age of gold for men of talent, there flourished a certain Alessandro, called after our custom Sandro, and further named Di Botticello, for a reason which we shall presently see. His father, Mariano Filipepi, a Florentine citizen, brought him up with care, and caused him to be instructed in all such things as are usually taught to children before they choose a calling. But although the boy readily mastered whatever he wished to learn, he was constantly discontented; neither would he take any pleasure in reading, writing or reckoning, so that the father, exasperated by his son's waywardness [the choice of words is a typical piece of Vasarian intolerance], apprenticed him in despair to a friend of his named Botticello, a goldsmith who was an able master of his craft. There was at that time a close and constant intercourse between the goldsmiths and the painters, and Sandro, who possessed considerable ingenuity, and was strongly disposed to the arts of design, became enamoured of painting and resolved to devote himself entirely to that vocation.'

There is no evidence of an apprenticeship to any goldsmith of that name in Florence; it is therefore more likely that Botticelli's name came from his brother Giovanni.

'He acknowledged his purpose at once to his father, and the latter, who knew the force of his inclinations, took him accordingly to the Carmelite monk, Fra' Filippo, who was a most excellent painter of that time, with whom he placed him to study the art, as Sandro himself had desired. Devoting himself thereupon entirely to the vocation he had chosen, Sandro so closely followed the directions and imitated the manner of his master, that Fra' Filippo conceived a great love for him, and instructed him so effectually, that Sandro rapidly attained to such a degree in art as none would have predicted for him.'

Apart from the reference on the first page to his apprenticeship with Lippi, the really important information which Vasari conveys here concerns Botticelli's restlessness and discontent as a student, and Vasari hints at it again later with his customary psychological penetration, referring to Botticelli as a *persona sofistica* (a refined and studious man). The dubious list of paintings given by Vasari can be ignored, as it is less important than the anecdotes, which, superficial as they are made to seem by the writer, give a better understanding of Botticelli's personality. If we turn for a moment to Vasari's life of Cosimo Rosselli, who was, with Botticelli, one of the painters who helped to decorate the Sistine Chapel, the reactions of Pope Sixtus IV to their work may help to bring to light Botticelli's discontent and basic unwillingness to adapt himself to the atmosphere in Rome: 'Cosimo sought to hide a deficiency of imagination and drawing by covering his work with the finest ultramarine and other bright colours. He embellished his picture with much gold; there were neither trees, grass, drapery nor cloud that was not touched with it. So he hoped to make the Pope, who was not very well versed in the art, believe that he merited the first prize. The day the paintings were to be unveiled, his was seen with the rest. Instead of taking pity on him, the other artists mocked and derided his work. But, in the end, they were the ones who were mocked, for those colours which Cosimo had invented so dazzled the eyes of the Holy Father, who understood very little about these things, that he reckoned Cosimo had done better than all the others. Thus, having given him the prize, he commanded that the others cover their works with the finest blue and gold that could be found, so that theirs would be equal in richness and colour to the paintings of Cosimo. So these wretched painters, in despair at having to satisfy the Pope's ignorance, set themselves to the task of undoing the good work they had done. As a result Cosimo was able to laugh at those who shortly before had made a fool of him.' Whether or not we believe in these grave consequences of the Holy Father's incomprehension, the worldly ostentation of Rome is expressed typically by Vasari's amused treatment of the subject. This was evidently an environment which was quite unacceptable to Botticelli's 'refined and studious' nature.

Returning to Vasari's life of Botticelli: 'Sandro was fond of joking, and often amused himself at the expense of his disciples and friends . . . A weaver of cloth once came to live close to Sandro, and this man erected eight looms, which, when all were at work, caused an intolerable din with the trampling of the weavers and the clang of the shuttles, so that poor Sandro was deafened with it, and produced such a trembling and shaking throughout the house, which was not too solidly built, that the painter could not continue his work or even remain in the house. He frequently requested his neighbour to put an end to his disturbance, but the latter replied that he would do what he pleased in his own house. Angered by this, Sandro had an enormous stone of great weight, more than would fill a waggon, placed in exact equilibrium on the wall of his own dwelling, which was higher than that of his neighbour, and not very strong; this stone threatened to fall at the slightest shake given to the wall, when it must have crushed the roof, floors, frames, and workmen of the weaver to atoms. Terrified, the man hastened to Sandro, who gave him his own reply in his own words, namely that he would do what he pleased in his own house; the weaver was compelled to come to reasonable terms, and to be a less troublesome neighbour.'

We find it further related, that Sandro Botticelli once, in jest, accused a friend of his own of heresy. When called before the judge, the accused naturally demanded to know by whom he was accused and of what. Being told that Sandro had declared him to hold the opinion of the Epicureans, that the soul dies with the body, he required that his accuser should be confronted with him before the judge. Sandro was summoned accordingly, and the accused man exclaimed: 'It is true that I hold the opinion stated respecting the soul of this man, who is a brute beast; is he not also a heretic, for without a grain of learning, scarcely knowing how to read, has he not undertaken to make a commentary on Dante, and take his name in vain?'

Both episodes are rather commonplace, though the final one is typical of the traditional tales of the period, from Sacchetti's *Novelle* to the tale of the Fat Woodcutter (*Il Grasso Legnaiolo*). And yet, viewed in the contest of Botticelli's last years, his sympathy with Savonarola and his sense of a tragic fate, the anecdotes acquire a deeper significance which was beyond Vasari's power to comprehend. The despair and affliction underlying these stories was ignored, and Vasari could only offer his usual sententious and basically unimaginative statement of the facts. 'This master is said to have had an extraordinary love for those whom he knew to be zealous students in art [here we have an example of Vasari's insight], and is affirmed to have earned considerable sums of money; but as he was a bad manager and very careless, all came to nothing. Finally, having become old, unfit for work, and helpless, he was obliged to go on crutches, being unable to stand upright, and so died, after long illness and decrepitude, in his seventy-eighth year.'

Works

Lippi, Pollaiolo and Verrocchio were the formative influences in the early years of Botticelli's career. This has been the view of modern criticism until recently. Verrocchio can be momentarily disregarded; his place in the early Quattrocento must remain doubtful until the corpus of his work has been more adequately studied. Both Pollaiolo and Lippi, however, are of immediate importance to our discussion: Pollaiolo was the last representative of the revolution in art during the early years of the fifteenth century; Lippi, with his acute faculty of perception, had investigated many of the problems that had survived from the amazing social and political revival which took place in Florence around 1460. Sandro's early association with these painters was not only an opportunity to develop formal inventiveness and enrich his style, it introduced him to the two great alternative systems of expression which were being developed from the study of Masaccio's art, the central theme of the century until the advent of Michelangelo.

Any reference to Sandro's development at this time involves the whole of the period around 1470, dominated by the aged Lippi, by Pollaiolo, still in the early stages of his maturity, and by the fledgling Leonardo; we can appreciate the importance of the Florentine absorption of early Renaissance influences. It should be remembered that in the preceding period both Masaccio and Brunelleschi based their beliefs on the autonomy of man (Giotto's view had been similar, as is now recognized by modern studies) and by implication accorded a similar autonomy to nature, implying hypothetically the existence of a natural reality which was a concrete and self-consistent value: nature was therefore, neither the exclusive domain of man's reason nor a manifestation of the divine will (the medieval 'daughter of God'). Brunelleschi in fact formulated perspective as a science of existence as well as vision: implying a concordance between man, who exists through his vision, and nature, which exists in the vision of man. The concept is clear enough, and is confirmed in Alberti's *Trattato della Pittura,* where these theoretical ideas were applied to colourful descriptions of complex landscapes for the instruction of artists. Some of these ideas are evident in certain landscape details of Masaccio's Carmine frescoes; they appear to prove the faultiness of certain widely held theories about the nature of early Renaissance art which place undue emphasis on man as the architect of his own fate, *faber fortunae suae* (of which Donatello's powerful figure of Gattamelata is considered an example), and consequently neglect the importance of the ideas of the early fathers of the Renaissance. This misunderstanding affects interpretations of Botticelli and his period: the so called 'heroic' influences of Brunelleschi, Donatello and Masaccio are emphasized to the detriment of the less obvious qualities which they share with, say, Domenico Veneziano. Again, Pollaiolo's 'Herculean' qualities have been emphasized, but his poetically rarified expression of nature has been largely ignored.

This critical view is understandable, since Florentine painters were obsessed with purely formal problems. Nevertheless, Domenico Veneziano's interpretation of Masaccio, in landscape particularly, was developed mainly outside Florence, by Piero della Francesca (one of the 'fathers' of the Renaissance, and, incidentally, of major importance to the landscape-based art of Venice). Domenico Veneziano, and his follower Alessio Baldovinetti, also influenced Antonio Pollaiolo, and the wider implications of Pollaiolo's art were later passed on to Leonardo. This development can clearly be traced back to Giotto, in whose work nature was incidental to the concept of man. In Masaccio, and even more in Domenico Veneziano, an equilibrium is maintained between human nature and the surrounding cosmos. Finally, in Pollaiolo, nature is the domain of Pan, while man is transformed into Hercules, and himself becomes a mythical creature. Leonardo, later in the century, developed the theme of man's position as an 'elemental' force of nature.

This line of development was also the most important for Botticelli between 1460-70, while Lippi's influence still survived as a contrary impulse. Lippi had elaborated his own elegant version of Masaccio's humanism, and of his interpretation of landscape; the *Madonna and Child with St John* in the Uffizi is the most transparently beautiful expression of this evolution of his style.

Lippi failed to understand the inner validity of Masaccio's perspective: space considered as an environment rationally organized by the action of man; reality made concrete and inalienable. Above all Masaccio had made perspective into a practical instrument with which to manipulate and collate his images. What Lippi did understand so well was the autonomous value of the human figure; he took advantage of his own spatial deficiencies, and concentrated on the plastic expression of his line, with the image tied to the plane of the picture. Landscape is pushed far back, almost as if seen through the wrong end of a telescope, and also tends to add to the isolation of the figures.

Of real importance here is the fact that Masaccio's and Brunelleschi's idea of man was once again in question. With the exclusion of a 'concrete' environment (present, however, in a narrative, descriptive way in Domenico Veneziano, and the austere geometric interiors of Andrea del Castagno) the image becomes symbolic and lyrically suggestive, and has no active or concrete reality.

The course open to Botticelli was a choice between two sets of ideas taken from a single source. Pollaiolo represented the intellectual naturalistic trend at its most refined. Lippi was basically a humanist, though there were fourteenth-century additions in his work: the sophisticated love poems of Guido (Cavalcanti) and even the allegorically complex *Divine Comedy* of Dante were used as sources for the introduction of transcendental concepts into his work. These currents of thought had another and deeper significance. They reflected a change, or decline, in the civic ideas which had been characteristic of the revolutionary early fourteenth century. The introduction to Alberti's *Trattato della Pittura* contains passages which theorize the new Romanism. The institutions of the present were considered to be as important as past achievements. Alberti in fact preferred the work of his friends to the antique masters; 'those dear friends of mine Nencio [Ghiberti], Luca and Masaccio', and above all 'Pippo the architect [Brunelleschi]'.

The *Apostles* and the *Prophets* of Masaccio and Donatello had a new significance in the role they accorded to
man, and the emphasis placed on individual responsibility
and self-determination, important political and public virtues. But private virtues, even the old courtly habits, were
coming into favour again, a tendency which was associated
in Florence with the rise of the Medici. Taste also declined:
Cosimo the Elder chose the feeble sub-Gothic architect
Michelozzo in place of Brunelleschi for the convent of San
Marco and the Ca' Fagiolo, and, just after the turn of the
century, Piero the Gouty employed the mediocre talent of
Benozzo Gozzoli to celebrate the Medici name in the chapel
of the Palazzo di Via Larga.

As courtly behaviour gradually became general in Florentine
society, the reaction against the austerity of the old customs
grew. Rich new private palaces were built; tournaments and
fairs (these show clearly the Medici influence on the taste
of the period) were paid for out of the money earned by the
merchants.

This changing situation was most closely reflected in the
visual arts, particularly the emblematic paintings of the
period, as we can see from Pollaiolo's work: the silver cross
made for the Baptistry in Florence, and the dancing, griffin-
or falcon-like figures on the walls of the Villa Gallina
are instances of these. Pisanello's *Eustachi* and the aristo-
cratic *Magi* of Gentile da Fabriano had been replaced by
these fiercely energetic figures placed against the blue and
gold of the coat of arms of the Medici. Into his landscapes
Pollaiolo introduces the antique figures of Hercules or Apol-
lo, more dashing perhaps than the real-life Federigo degli
Alberighi, but basically not very different from him in their
attitudes. The enlightened Signoria of the Medici served in
fact to further the social, political and cultural decline of
Florence. Worldly elegance and intellectual refinement were
encouraged in the place of individual and public virtue. An
almost medieval state of affairs was re-established, though
enriched by the extraordinary cultural experience of the
early years of the century.

In drawing his stylistic conclusions from the artistic wealth
of the previous era Botticelli was bound to feel the appeal

of Lippi's lyrical individuality. Lippi's painting, in its allusion to an ideal, was in line with the neo-Platonism favoured by the Medici court. We have also seen that it retained and revived medieval characteristics wh.c'. were in keeping with the courtly manners reintroduced into public life by the Medici.

Having summarized thus briefly the prevailing cultural climate, we can turn to Botticelli's early works; the *Fortitude* of the Mercatanzia, 1470 (*pl. 9*), and the *St Sebastian,* in Berlin (*pl. 15*), which was previously dated, from an ancient source, 1474, and thought to have been painted for the church of Santa Maria Maggiore. It is not surprising that some stylistic confusion is evident in these early works. A plastic, linear movement derived from Pollaiolo is introduced into the more congenial Lippesque themes. As for landscape, the full implications of Pollaiolo's style have not been understood, and so it retains a secondary, purely decorative function in Botticelli's work.

The immediate consequence of Botticelli's choice of models is a refusal to consider perspective as an aid to representation, or as a basis for architectonic structure. Furthermore it involves the rejection of the idea of the man-nature relationship, though in a more drastic way than had ever occurred to Lippi, who in any case lacked the ability to see the full implications of his own style. To quote Leonardo, who immediately understood Botticelli, ' Sandro, why do you place the third thing before the second? ' and, ' To one who does not love landscape it seems a subject unworthy of study, as our Botticelli said. '

The opposition between Pollaiolo and Botticelli can now be considered. Pollaiolo's work was so rich in possibilities that it was perhaps the most fruitful source of inspiration for Michelangelo and the early mannerist painters of Florence. Botticelli's earliest influence was through his contact with Lippi, as a student; ' he was taken to Filippo ... an excellent painter of that time, and taught there in the master's own style' (Vasari). The impact of Pollaiolo's work is felt later. During this first period Botticelli produced a number of works which are variations of Lippi's *Madonna* in the Uffizi: *Innocenti Madonna* (*pl. 1*), *Fesch*

Madonna (*pl. 2*), *Madonna della Loggia* in the Uffizi, the *Guidi Madonna* in the Louvre, and the *Madonna* of the Accademia (*pl. 3*), the *Madonna del Roseto* in the Louvre, the *Duveen Madonna* in New York, and the *Corsini Madonna* in Washington.

These works show signs of Lippi's influence both in their thematic treatment and in their development of line and colour; while their subject-matter shows traces of the influence of Andrea Verrocchio's studio, which Botticelli may possibly have frequented after leaving Lippi.

The contribution of Verrocchio's studio to the development of Florentine painting between 1460 and 1470 is a complex question. Briefly, the source of 'Verrocchian' influence seems to lie not in Verrocchio himself but in an unknown artist. This 'Pseudo-Verrocchio' painted a series of panels, including a *Pietà,* now lost, which was signed, through a curious error on the part of some old restorer, 'Ant. Pollaioli'; the tabernacle in the Via del Campanile; *The Three Archangels* in the Uffizi; the *St Monica* in the church of Santo Spirito; and two panels in the Accademia representing *St Monica* and *St Augustine*. The Pseudo-Verrocchio is also presumed to be responsible for the pre-Leonardo portions of the *Baptism* in the Uffizi, although Ragghianti maintains that these are at least partly the work of Botticelli.

According to Mesnil, *The Three Archangels* was painted not later than 1467, and in my opinion this picture constitutes the true point of contact between Botticelli and the Pseudo-Verrocchio. It presents characteristics which are fundamental to Botticelli's creative style at the time when it was painted: the enhanced linear rhythms of the figure of Gabriel are post-Lippi in style, and the non-perspectival character of the landscape, which is basically inspired by Pollaiolo, enables the figures to be placed in isolation and emphasized. The effect is of a set-piece in which Lippi's ideas have been deliberately used and then refined upon by Botticelli. He has managed to instil into his line a descriptive quality which the friar never possessed. This development from the simple Lippi motive is carried a step further in a group of works (the *Madonnas* now in London, Naples and

14

Strasbourg) in which the composition is articulated and connects the figures with increased effectiveness. In the *Madonna and Child with two Angels* (*pls. 4-5*) the figures are grouped in an enclosed garden, and in the background, emphasized by an arrangement of trees, there is a rhythmically stylized landscape.

However, the influence of Pollaiolo was of vital importance in the move towards linear purity. Previously he had shown a tendency, through Lippi, to model his forms stiffly and in a rather dry relief reminiscent of Verrocchio. His figures now began to lose their inherent weight and become more expressive. This tendency is contradicted, however, in certain works painted under Pollaiolo's influence before the *St Sebastian* in Berlin; the *Fortitude* (*pl. 9*) and the *Holofernes* and *Judith* diptych in the Uffizi (*pls. 13-14*). These two works have harshly-modelled forms which again show a rather academic approach to Verrocchio. Botticelli's reaction to the lingering influences of his early period resulted in a further step in his stylistic development. Themes begin to appear in the paintings which point to his later style. Movement is explored as an externally expressed linear quality differing entirely from the latent energy and movement in Pollaiolo. Apart from the *Madonna and Saints* in the Uffizi, probably painted for the convent of Santa Elisabetta delle Convertite (*pls. 10-12*), the complex compositions of other works have a metallic quality, and linear flexibility is only occasionally evident; although this particular linear character is predominant in the Hutton portrait and the one in the Pitti (*pl. 8*).

Considering Botticelli's work as a series of successive periods, it must be admitted that we meet with certain apparent inconsistencies of style. The relative complexity of composition is often the cause of stylistic confusion. In compositions which are basically architectonic, such as the *Madonna and Saints* (*pls. 10-12*), the artist still has difficulty in using line as a structural element. He finds it easier to introduce line into paintings of simple contruction and single forms, such as portraits where the figure is placed against an abstract background. His stylistic ideas now run counter to those of his former master Lippi. His works of this period represent a stylistic compromise between Verrocchio and Pollaiolo, and already hint at an individual pictorial language of his own. We do not know whether he realized very clearly the implications of the work of Pollaiolo. At any rate he showed more interest in Pollaiolo's experimental, non-religious approach than in Lippi's humanism. Though he was probably unaware of it, Lippi's paintings did in fact hold possibilities for religious and mystical expression by means of allegories. In any case it is fairly obvious that his personal development at this time was dictated more by instinctive feeling than by any critical assessment of the stylistic influences around him. Intuition was of more use to him than speculation as a means of understanding the nature of ideal reality. In fact a continual refinement of intuition runs parallel to his development as a painter, and in this way he sensed the implications of both neo-Platonism and the later movement led by Savonarola. Formal problems of the early period were no longer a preoccupation to him. Before considering the *St Sebastian* in Berlin, which marks the peak of his maturity, we should examine the *Adoration of the Magi* in the National Gallery, London. The problems of documentation and of dating are considerable. The date suggested by Salvini (in his 'Note sul Botticelli', 1962) seems the most plausible; an earlier one would place it out of step with the line of development followed so far. Salvini claims four characteristics of note: 'awkward composition and timid execution, Lippi's influence especially in the upper portion, pointing to the early style of Botticelli, *c.* 1465; the presence of certain figures showing Pollaiolo's influence, belonging to Botticelli's style shortly after 1470; and, finally, parts by the hand of Filippino: it is known that Filippino was working in Botticelli's workshop in 1472. This painting was therefore planned and begun by Botticelli in Filippo Lippi's studio about 1465-66, and for this reason may be considered one of Botticelli's earliest works, painted immediately after the earlier variations on Lippi's famous *Madonna.* It was left unfinished and continued later by Botticelli with Filippino's help. His young pupil was given a free hand in the painting of heads and figures, though not permitted to interfere by correcting or over-painting. The date 1470 seems reliable, judging from the presence of Filippino (this pupil probably entered the studio some time before 1472), and from the more fully developed figures in the composition, which were painted entirely by Botticelli in the final phase of the work. These are definitely Pollaiolesque figures corresponding to the period of the so-called *Man with the Medal,* and the *Judith* diptych, which anticipates the *St Sebastian* of 1473-4.'

In style the *St Sebastian* can be more closely related to Pollaiolo than any other of Botticelli's paintings. It also shows the emergence of an individual pictorial language. The reciprocal influences of Botticelli and Pollaiolo are again present: line, however functional, accentuates the two-dimensional quality of the image, so that the figure is on the same plane as the background. The general effect is melodic and consists of a play of precise colour zones without emphasis on movement and space (*pl. 15*). Masaccio's contribution to art was being evolved by Pollaiolo into a new painting of nature in evolution; overt physical action replaces the action latent in Masaccio. Pollaiolo believed in *homo sive natura sive deus* (man=nature=god), and his art was built up on this concept; no doubt he hoped that his work might become the expression of a personal religion of nature. Historical developments in painting meant nothing to Botticelli: action was a quality to be transformed into contemplation, and myth the natural vehicle through which this could be achieved.

Like Botticelli, Lippi was unaffected by the historical implications of Masaccio's work. Lippi's art, among the trends and creative possibilities of the time, was only significant for the freedom and extravagance of its expression. The *Judith* diptych (*pls. 13-14*) is an example of a work in which, even prior to the *St Sebastian,* we can observe true Botticellian characteristics. This is a representation of the discovery of Holofernes' body and the pensive return of Judith to Betulia. Action is ignored, and everything is concentrated into a contemplation of the melancholy of the irrevocable.

If we now examine the mythical content of Botticelli's and Pollaiolo's works we shall notice that in the myth of

Pollaiolo time is natural, not historical; action is co-extensive with space. Hercules can therefore appear suddenly, like an essence of nature. With Botticelli there is no need for an illusion of space and action; there is simply time which is an ideal dimension. Moral truth and beauty, the individual and the cosmos are united – though much later his work changes and the subjects become identified with the tragic fate of the divinity.

There is a series of portraits, datable about the time of the *St Sebastian*, in which the single-figure-and-background theme is refined still further: the *Man with the Medal of Cosimo the Elder* (*pl. 16*), the *Profile Portrait of a Woman* (*pl. 18*), a modulation of lyrical line and muted colours, and the portraits of *Lorenzo* and *Giuliano de' Medici* (*pl. 17*). Slightly later (*c.* 1476) in the *Adoration of the Magi* (*pls. 19-23*), Pollaiolesque linear inflections are deliberately diminished. We should notice here that throughout these works space and perspective are progressively eliminated still further. Traditional perspective is still used in the *Convertite Madonna* (*pls. 10-12*), though in the *Adoration* tondo in the National Gallery, London (contemporary with the last stages of the other London *Adoration*), perspective and space are only a lyrical suggestion. In this tondo the setting which surrounds the figures is partly hidden by the spreading of the group in the central foreground. The classical ruins have become timelessly symbolic, typical therefore of Botticelli's classicism up until his last works. In the Uffizi *Adoration* there is a much greater effort towards linear consistency of style, rhythmically linking and binding the ruins and figures together; the effect is to turn the whole scene into an ideal allegory outside time. This is a strictly historical work, painted for the Medici family and intended as an exaltation of the artist's patrons, but the portrait figures of Cosimo, Giovanni, Lorenzo and Giuliano, and Botticelli himself, introduce a mood of absolute contemplation.

By the time of the Uffizi *Adoration,* and in particular the *Madonna of the Sea* in the Accademia, Florence (*pls. 24-5*), derivations of detail and structural form from Pollaiolo have been absorbed into a serene and confidently poetical style, in which he was able to express his concepts without effort. Next in chronological order is the *Spring* (*pls. 26-32*), one of Botticelli's greatest poetic achievements, in which he identifies himself completely with one of the main idealistic preoccupations of his work so far, Ficino's neo-Platonism.

Vasari's description of the subject is splendid although inadequate: '*Venus, accompanied by the Graces adorned with flowers, announcing Spring*'. However, it is similar to the suggestion put forward by Warburg; that the *Spring* represents the realm of Venus, inhabited by eternal spring, and he also believes that the idea is derived from Poliziano. It is impossible to cover all the hypotheses that have been put forward; the reader may, if he wishes, consult Salvini's thorough analysis (1962), which follows that of Gombrich (1945), who suggests that the painting is a celebration of the virtue of *humanitas,* taken from the philosopher Ficino. Gombrich also maintains that Poliziano's poetry is the link here between Ficino and Botticelli.

Salvini sums up: 'Poliziano is not Ficino; his poetry softens the harsh character of neo-Platonism; there is a sweet, fresh idyllic quality in it which is touched with a nostalgia for an antiquity which he admires (though not without a touch of subtle mockery) as the place where the senses and the spirit keep their eternal youth. This explains why, in Botticelli's representation of Venus as *humanitas* and spirit of universal love, the traditional meaning of Venus as the goddess of love and pleasure is not completely ignored. And also why, on the right hand side, the allegory begins with an allusion to the erotic myth of Flora and Zephyr, while on the left it concludes with the skyward-gazing figure of Mercury (signifying Reason and Knowledge). Venus, therefore, is *humanitas,* the virtue which comes from universal love (which Ficino considered the motive force of the world). This platonic love envelops and sublimates earthly love. Man's soul, according to Ficino, is divided through its double attraction both to God and to the body. "By a certain natural instinct it ascends to the heights and descends to the depths (*naturali quodam instinctu ascendit ad supera, discendit ad infera*)", and so even when attracted

to the body the soul is linked with its essence, and therefore
" free from moral reproof " (O. Kristeller: *Il pensiero filo-
sofico di Marsilio Ficino,* Firenze, 1953). Venus then, like
the human soul, is centrally placed, flanked by earthly love
(Zephyr and Flora), the serene happiness of the Hour (Flora
transformed into Venus by Spring), Beauty (the Graces
between Delight and ambivalent Love), and the source
of the intellectual contemplation of God (Mercury). Venus
therefore incarnates the Platonic virtue of *humanitas* without discarding any of the attributes as the goddess of Love.'
It may now be easy to see how Botticelli's contemplative
non-historical form of art had developed at this point into
a suitable instrument by which contemporary neo-Platonism
might be interpreted. And also that his encounter with Ficino and Poliziano had been a logical consequence of tend-
encies reaching far back in time. From a strictly formal
point of view the *Spring* is the final confirmation of the
type of pictorial organization noted in his works so far. Space
is eliminated and nature is dematerialized into Idea. A
linear rhythm running through the whole image is
brought into the foreground, and the modulation of colour
is carefully balanced. Contemporary with this supreme poetic achievement we have the *St Augustine* in the church
of Ognissanti (*pl. 33*), dated aproximately 1480, in which
Botticelli reintroduces the traditional theme of a solidly
constructed architectural perspective. A heaviness and angu-
larity in the anatomy, characteristic of the plastic style of
Andrea del Castagno, suggests that Sandro might have been
interested in Castagno's work since 1478, at which time he
was commissioned to paint, on the side of the Palazzo Vecchio, the Pazzi conspirators who had been hanged after the
unsuccessful plot which had resulted in the death of Giuliano de' Medici. Botticelli may have been impressed by similar figures of the Albizi in the fresco by Andrea del Castagno on the Bargello, but it seems unlikely that he could have
been influenced by a style so out of keeping with his own.
And in fact, in the *St Augustine* we see that the cramped
architectural surrounding has the effect of eliminating
space *ab initio,* the saint's legs have no possibility of being
in full perspective, and the cornice above appears to be cut

20

short at one end. Line and colour superimposition, rather than chiaroscuro, is used to give plasticity. A preferable source for this work is perhaps the *St Jerome with a headless female saint* in the church of St Domenico di Pistoia, attributed variously to Pollaiolo and Verrocchio, but which, in the author's opinion, probably comes from the studio of the Pseudo-Verrocchio mentioned previously. This interpretation is further supported by the *Annunciation of San Martino alla Scala (pls. 34-5)*, painted in 1485, a year later than the *St Augustine*. Here again the perspective is compressed in the foreground of the painting, and the distant landscape behind has no connection with any vanishing point. The linear contorsions in the figures have increased, bringing to mind the late period, in which serene and tragic elements, as well as allegorically sacred and profane subjects, alternate and conflict. We can however see in the figure of the angel which descends softly from above, and in the rhythmic curve of the Virgin as she bends modestly forward, something of the crystalline purity of *Spring.* Perhaps it would not be too fanciful to sense in these contrasts the first hints of an approaching storm.

Botticelli was in Rome between June 1471 and September 1482. He was summoned there by Pope Sixtus IV to decorate the walls of the Sistine Chapel, with Ghirlandaio, Cosimo Rosselli and Perugino (later joined by Signorelli, Pinturicchio and Piero di Cosimo). This can be thought of as a break in Botticelli's career. He painted three frescoes of a narrative cycle, depicting scenes from the Old and New Testaments: *The Trials of Moses, The Temptation of Christ (pls. 37-9)* and *The Punishment of the Rebel Angels.* The requirements on Botticelli in Rome were hardly suited to his spiritual disposition: the frescoes were expected to be monumental and naturalistic in execution, and appropriate therefore to the contemporary environment of Rome. In effect, they were allegories of narrative type, in a naturalistic treatment, and, as such, required a creative approach totally different to that which produced the *Spring,* where allegory is the result of a process of abstraction without historical references of any kind. The Roman frescoes were intended to be realistically suggestive of space, action and historical fact, and in consequence Sandro was only able to express individuality in a few details, such as the *Daughter of Jethro* in the *Trials of Moses,* and the *Girl carrying Wood* in the *Temptation of Christ.*

It has been suggested that Botticelli's first encounter with the ruins of ancient Rome, and therefore with the world of antiquity, was a decisive factor in his future development. This is hardly likely. It seems more probable that the artist found Roman remains depressingly solemn rather than monumental and impressive. The head of the Uffizi *Centaur* (although a common bas-relief motif in Roman sarcophagi) is really derived from the solid and colourful plastic values of Antonio and Piero del Pollaiolo, as exemplified in the three *Saints* by these artists in the church of San Miniato, the *Virtues* in the Mercatanzia, and the London *St Sebastian,* works in which Antonio's obsession with human anatomy is replaced by a more freely relaxed manner. The frescoes for the Villa Tornabuoni-Lemmi, which are now in the Louvre, were probably executed shortly after Botticelli's return from Rome, and are additional proof that the artist's experience in Rome was of little importance to his stylistic formation. The subjects portrayed are Lorenzo Tornabuoni standing in front of a group of figures symbolizing the Liberal Arts (*pl. 42*), and Venus who is offering gifts to a young girl (*pls. 43-5*). The line is fluent and melodic, flowing through the figures grouped in a space which is without depth, while the setting as a whole has no particular reference to a specific historical time. Here we can see that the painter has gladly returned to a conception of allegory, sublimating beauty and idea, which was entirely natural to him. On closer inspection a growing sadness of mood is evident in these works, particularly in the *Pallas.* This tendency was already latent in the Berlin *St Sebastian,* possibly accounting for the rather harsh stylistic treatment of this work, and results in a further loss of the equilibrium which had been so wonderfully captured in the *Spring.* The spiritual style of the period to which the *Spring* belongs is revived and taken a step further in a last group of works which are among the most delightful of Botticelli's entire production: the *Madonna of the Magnificat,* Uffizi (*pls. 48-*

9), the *Madonna and Child,* Museo Poldi Pezzoli, Milan (*pls. 50-1*), the *Venus and Mars,* National Gallery, London (*pl. 52*), and lastly the *Birth of Venus* (*pls. 53-5*). All these are new allegorical variations which reinterpret and elaborate the poetic concepts of neo-Platonism.

The force of Botticelli's rarefied 'secular' idealism was in no way attenuated by its further exploitation in these works, all of which belong to the period between 1482-85. In them Botticelli's neo-Platonism was dialectically reinforced by the introduction of a new vein of religious feeling. The neo-Platonic idealism of his former period was intensified to the point of identifying Idea with Divinity. The ideal and the real world are reconciled in the concept of Redemption. Allegory succeeds in transforming the world of reality; it does this by seeking the divine in man, a state typified in the serene equilibrium inherent in the identification of Virtue with Beauty, a point where all activity ceases, which in consequence constitutes a revelation of God and his work. Early Renaissance thought had been entirely different in its approach, seeking the link between God, man and nature in man's reason, and his active life. Botticelli, proceeding from Filippo Lippi's humanism, moves into the realm of the divine and the Idea; in the dialogue between God and Man which is the theme of the Redemption he finds the theme of his last period. Botticelli's approach has been called medieval, but in fact medieval transcendentalism is replaced in his thought by the idea of reason as the source of divine knowledge. His work remains, side by side with the experimentalism of Leonardo da Vinci, one of the essential achievements of the Renaissance – and this is confirmed by the fact that many of the stylistic and conceptual innovations of the 'divine' Michelangelo can ultimately be traced back to Botticelli.

The philosophical sadness which we saw in the *Pallas* is predominant in all the paintings of this period, 1482-85.

As the Idea becomes purer, man finds himself further from Elysium. In the *Madonna of the Magnificat* (*pls. 48-9*) this ultimate, pellucid perfection is symbolized in a circular composition. The abstract quality of the work is expressed perfectly in its elusive linear rhythms. The approachable

Virgins of Lippi have given way to a cold personification of abstract Love, a Platonic footnote to the Canticles.

The allegory of *Venus and Mars* (*pl. 52*) is perhaps an interpretation of Botticelli's own private world. Mars is lying inert on the ground, head thrown back as if overcome by the idea of Beauty. Venus lies near, but she is abstract, an unapproachable absolute being in a timeless world. This sense of absolute being is perfectly expressed in the *Birth of Venus,* which in its poetic intensity surpasses anything imagined by Poliziano. The nature of this work recalls the hypothesis concerning the soul in the philosophy of Ficino: the soul is suspended between *supera* and *infera* (the heights and the depths), between intelligence (concomitant with faith) and the material world. Here, I think, Argan's words are appropriate: 'This beautiful female form, with its diaphanous shapes and pure outlines, constitutes a rejection or a sublimation of its physical aspect. It is like a challenge on the part of the intellect – a challenge thrown in the face of sensuality.' Or we might say that by sublimation in Idea, matter and being are converted into intellect. We are now able to appreciate the relationship between Botticelli and Pollaiolo, and on a different level Leonardo. The opposition is basically that between idealism and empiricism. For Leonardo and Pollaiolo divinity is latent in matter, eluding its transcendence through action; for Botticelli matter is transfigured into intellect and contemplation, and finally Idea (*pls. 53-5*).

In the *Santo Spirito Altarpiece,* painted in 1485, now in Berlin, non-Christian, neo-Platonic subjects have been replaced by Christian themes. Tragic and anguished feelings become more evident. The style is agitated, so that the rhythmic perfection achieved in the *Venus* is destroyed. It seems as if the long-prepared crisis has finally erupted into both style and subject. The two worn and emaciated Saints on either side of the slender figure of the Virgin seem to oppress the infant Christ, and stand as symbols, at the same time, of the Annunciation and the Apocalypse. St John the Baptist and St John the Evangelist are allegorical symbols of the Redemption, and also prefigure the coming end of the world. Here the line is tense and burdened with *angst.*

Slightly later in date, the *Madonna of the Pomegranate* (*pls. 56-7*) can be considered a further variation on the theme of the *Magnificat.* The supremely poised beauty of the Madonna has a languor which comes close to expressing despair. This work is the lyrical expression of Botticelli's anguished maturity, though in his struggle for intense emotional effect the abstract, almost frigid, ideal perfection of previous works is somehow lost.

The *San Barnaba Altarpiece* (*pls. 58-9*), painted perhaps soon after the *Madonna of the Pomegranate,* follows the *Santo Spirito Altarpiece* in style. Its striking characteristic is again the ascetic emaciation and forlornness of the Saints (St John staring sadly out in an attitude of bewilderment). The sorrowful tension has had the effect of hardening the formerly rhythmic line, and brings to mind something of the preoccupations of the mannerist painters of a later period. But perhaps the architecture is the most significant, for decorative elements taken from natural forms are eliminated, and it thus departs from anything seen previously in Botticelli's work. In the *Santo Spirito Altarpiece* embellishments of this sort had still been used: three small niches, which emphasized its triptychal form, each containing a small decorative shrub. Here we have only a sumptuous apse, a heroic rostrum on which the Holy Mother and Child are raised above the faithful. This triumphal architecture represents an important moment of transition, Botticelli's final rejection of his concern for the sublimation of natural beauty, via the intellect. It stands as the painter's release from a vow; after it he joined the band of ' weepers ' who followed Savonarola.

His attraction to Savonarola was no doubt as spontaneous as the one he had previously conceived for neo-Platonism and Ficino. In other words, it is more likely that he voluntarily joined Savonarola's group of followers than that the friar's preaching merely influenced him. It may well have seemed an answer to many of the doubts which had preoccupied him since 1485. It is reasonable to assume that Sandro found a relief in Savonarola's sermons, from the formal and conceptual problems involved in the creation of previous paintings such as the *San Barnaba Altarpiece*. Certainly, the connection with Savonarola was the source of the bare undecorated style of his last works: the *Annunciation* in the Uffizi (*pls. 60-1*), the *Lehman Annunciation* (*pl. 63*), the *St Augustine in his Cell* (*pl. 64*), the *Lamentations* in Munich (*pl. 66*) and Milan (*pl. 67*), the *Calumny* (*pls. 70-2*), the *Stories of Lucretia and Virginia* (*pl. 73*), the *Mystic Nativity* in London (*pl. 74*), and the *Crucifixion* in the Fogg Art Museum, Cambridge, Mass.

These works of Botticelli's last period form a progression from the theme of communion with the Deity (*St Augustine in his Cell*) to that of sacred drama (the *Mystic Nativity*) in which man is reduced to the role of an agonized spectator, able only to contemplate and pray. Hence the sense of desolation and helplessness in some of the individual figures in these compositions: the figures around Christ in the *Lamentation* scenes in the Milan and Munich paintings (*pls. 66-7*), the angels who sense an impending tragedy and embrace in the foreground of the *Nativity,* and the Magdalen who clutches the cross in the strange allegorical *Crucifixion* in the Fogg Art Museum.

Calumny (*pls. 70-2*) differs in some respects from the works just mentioned. Its story is the well-known one told by Lucian, of Apelles, the young man who was dragged by Calumny into the presence of Penitence and Truth. The story alludes to the impotence of man in the sight of evil. He is again a spectator. Argan, referring to the central group which includes the figure of Calumny, interprets the ceaseless movement as an allusion to eternal repetition, and suggests that the ornate hall in which the scene takes place is symbolic of ' a distant region containing the deep motives for man's action and the source of his ideas.' *Calumny* depicts man as a creature with intellect and feeling, but lacking Grace. He is also powerless. Without Redemption, he is powerless to achieve Justice.

In the last period allegory was still Botticelli's authentic spiritual mode of expression, as it had been throughout his career. Not surprisingly, at this time, from about 1490, he turned also to illustrations, commissioned by Lorenzo di Pierfranco, interpreting the *Commedia* of Dante. The historical importance of these allegories should not be overlooked;

for one thing their tormented lyricism and sensitive introspection were to become a source of inspiration to Florentine artists during the early mannerist period.

It is sad to think that at the end of Botticelli's life his fellow-citizens turned their backs on him, preferring the work of younger men, even products of his own studio such as Filippino. The Florentine agent of that arch-intellectual Isabella Gonzaga reported to his mistress that 'Allessandro Botechiella' was the only painter not burdened with commissions, and that he would 'gladly work for her.'

Botticelli and the Critics

In the brief review of Botticelli's life at the front of this book I suggested that, owing to his inability to respond to the painter's personality, Vasari failed him as a critic. We can imagine that Vasari was in some ways indifferent to Botticelli's work, which must have seemed archaic to him, and in its late period positively 'Gothic'. Certainly his painting did not fit in with the cultural interests of Vasari's own age. As has been suggested, the formal linear elements of Botticelli's art, and, on a deeper level, his anti-classical spirit, may have exercised an influence on the emergent personality of Michelangelo and on mannerism. In fact, this influence can be considered one of the vital links between the cultures of the Quattrocento and the Cinquecento, as meaningful as the connection between Pollaiolo's approach to landscape and Leonardo's investigations into the nature of natural phenomena. Of course, modern art history takes a wider view than Vasari, who shared the view of his time, in believing that all art was a continual evolution 'from Greek (Byzantine) to Latin (Roman)', from Giotto to the classicism of Michelangelo. The reaction against Botticelli in his own lifetime is perhaps understandable in the light of developments current in the early years of the sixteenth century, Botticelli's last active period; Leonardo and Michelangelo had already executed the *Cascina* and *Anghiari Cartoons,* which were introducing painters to new pictorial ideas.

The neglect of Botticelli persisted without interruption (even Lanzi's favourable criticism failed to stimulate interest in the painter), until his revival by the Pre-Raphaelites in the second half of the nineteenth century. Their appreciation of Botticelli, like that of other aesthetes of the period, was limited to the formal refinements of his style, and ignored the significance of the work as an expression of ideas. In fact Botticelli was normally, and very inappropriately, considered a primitive, except by Ruskin, who sensed the deep moral content pervading his work.

The immense volume of contemporary criticism of his work begins with Berenson, who examined the value of line and movement as they occurred in the paintings and the relation of the work to the whole Quattrocento period. Subsequent studies of value include: H. Ulmann, *Sandro Botticelli* (Munich 1893), the first fully-documented account of Botticelli's career; H. Horne, *Alessandro Filipepi Commonly Called Sandro Botticelli* (London 1908); W. Bode, *Botticelli* (Berlin 1921) and *Botticelli* (Stuttgart 1926); Schmarsow, *Sandro del Botticello* (Dresden 1923); Y. Yashiro, *Sandro Botticelli* (London 1925); A. Venturi, *Botticelli* (Rome 1925); G. Gamba, *Botticelli* (London 1937 and London 1947); S. Bettini, *Botticelli* (Bergamo 1924 and 1947); H. E. Gombrich, ' Botticelli's Mythologies ' in *Journal of the Warburg and Courtauld Institutes* (London 1945); G. C. Argan, *Botticelli* (Geneva 1957); R. Salvini, *Botticelli* (Milan 1958), and ' Note sul Botticelli ' and ' Interpretazioni politiche e interpretazioni filosofiche di alcune allegorie botticelliane ', both in *Scritti di storia dell'arte in onore di Mario Salmi* (Rome 1962).

Notes on the Plates

1 Madonna and Child with an Angel. Panel, 60 × 87 cm. Florence, Ospedale degli Innocenti, Pinacoteca. Formerly attributed by Cavalcaselle to Lippi, then to Botticelli by Ulmann, and later also by Bode, Gamba, Berenson, and Salvini. Doubtful are: Van Marle and Bettini. Opposed are: Venturi and Mesnil.

2 Madonna and Child with an Angel. Panel, 70×110 cm. Ajaccio, Musée Fesch. Attributed to Botticelli by Berenson. Like all other works of 1465-70, this panel shows the influence of Lippi.

3 Madonna and Child with Young St John and Two Angels. Panel, 62 × 85 cm. Florence, Galleria dell'Accademia. Originally in Santa Maria Nuova, then in the Uffizi, and in 1919 removed to the Accademia. First ascribed to Botticelli by Bode, then by Ulmann, Schmarsow, Van Marle, Gamba, Berenson, Procacci, and Salvini. Ascribed by Horne and Venturi to the 'school of Botticelli'.

4 Madonna and Child with Two Angels. Panel, 71×100 cm. Naples, Galleria Nazionale di Capodimonte. The original attribution is by Bode, accepted by the majority of critics (Schmarsow, Yashiro, Gamba, Berenson, L. Venturi, Mesnil, Bettini, Davies, and Salvini), rejected by Horne.

5 Madonna and Child with Two Angels. Detail.

6 Madonna and Child with Cherubim. Panel, 65×120 cm. Florence, Uffizi. Bode's ascription to Botticelli is favoured by the majority of critics. Stylistically in the manner of Lippi and Verrocchio, with lyrical overtones and a developing linear technique.

7 Madonna and Child against a Rose Hedge. Panel, 64 × 124 cm. Florence, Uffizi. Bode ascribes this panel to Botticelli, and suggests a date slightly before 1470. His opinion is shared by most critics.

8 Portrait of a Young Man. Panel. Florence, Pitti. Traditionally ascribed to Andrea del Castagno (accepted by Cavalcaselle and Morelli), then to Piero di Cosimo by Schmarsow. The inclusion of the painting in Venturi's Botticelli list was accepted by Bode. Later Venturi attributed it to the school of Filippo Lippi. Botticelli's authorship is not accepted by Ulmann; Kühnel ascribes it to Botticelli, Van Marle to 'a friend of Sandro's', and Berenson to Ghirlandaio's workshop. Berenson later acknowledged its authenticity. Modern criticism agrees unanimously on Botticelli and dates the work around 1470.

9 Fortitude. Panel, 87×167 cm. Florence, Uffizi. This panel belongs to a series of seven Virtues intended as decorations for the backs of seats, or an ornamental wainscoting, in the Court of the Mercatanzia. Piero del Pollaiolo had already completed a figure of Charity for the same guild in 1469, probably in competition with Verrocchio, and afterwards was given the full commission. In May 1470 Tommaso Soderini, Botticelli's patron and close friend of Lorenzo il Magnifico, succeded in obtaining for him a commission for two more virtues, for one of which, the *Fortitude*, Sandro received payment in August of the same year. Eventually the second of these two virtues was again given to Piero. The whole series is now on view in one room in the Uffizi. A firm dating for the *Fortitude* is a determinant factor in any analysis of Botticelli's early style. The influence of Pollaiolo is predominant, as would be expected, and the context of style is Verrocchio. We agree with Salvini who considers Lippi, Verrocchio and Pollaiolo the artists who had a continuing influence on Botticelli's style. This view is also held by Yashiro, Bettini and Argan.

10 Madonna and Child with Saints. Panel; 194 × 170 cm. Florence, Uffizi. Formerly in the church of Sant'Ambrogio all'Accademia, could be identified as the panel painted by Botticelli for the Augustinian nuns of Santa Maria delle Convertite (mentioned by Antonio Billi, an anonymous critic of Gaddi, Vasari and Borghini). It was attributed to Andrea del Castagno by Cavalcaselle though later critics have all affirmed Botticelli's authorship and dated it about 1470.

11 Madonna and Child with Saints. Detail: the head of the Virgin.

12 Madonna and Child with Saints. Detail: St Catherine.

13 Holofernes found Dead. Panel, 25×31 cm. Florence, Uffizi. A small diptych panel, the companion piece being the *Judith* (*pl.* 14). It was presented to Bianca Cappello by Rodolfo Sirigatti (mentioned by Borghini), and inherited by her son, Don Antonio de' Medici. On the latter's death it went to the Uffizi. Its attribution to Botticelli by Borghini is unanimously accepted, though disagreement exists as to its dating, generally accepted as slightly after 1470, except by Yashiro and Bettini, who prefer slightly before 1470.

14 Judith. Panel, 24×31 cm. Florence, Uffizi.

15 St Sebastian. Panel, 75×195 cm. Berlin, Staatliche Museen. Attributed to Botticelli by Cavalcaselle. It is almost certainly the work described by the anonymous critic previously mentioned as being in Santa Maria Maggiore ('a panel of St Sebastian against a column, which was painted in January 1473'). The date is consonant with its Pollaiolesque style.

16 Portrait of a Man with the Medal of Cosimo the Elder.
Panel, 44×57.5 cm. Florence, Uffizi. The attribution to Botticelli is
by Morelli and universally accepted, except by Bode. Efforts have
been made to identify the subject of this portrait with various
members of the Medici family; Piero the Gouty, Giovanni di Cosimo
and Piero di Lorenzo have been suggested at various times, but
all these identifications seem unacceptable on chronological grounds.
The date for the work is a matter of controversy, but we are
inclined to accept Salvini's, which is *c*. 1473-4.

17 Portrait of Giuliano de' Medici. Panel, 36 × 54 cm. Bergamo,
Accademia Carrara. There are three other versions of this portrait:
in the Crespi collection, Milan, the Staatliche Museen, and the Kress
Foundation, National Gallery, Washington. The prototype of the four
remains doubtful: in our view it is perhaps the Crespi portrait
which in relation to the other three has the figure in reverse,
matching with the portrait of Lorenzo now in the Lazzaroni collection in Paris. The authorities for the attribution of the four
portraits to Botticelli are as follows: for the one at Bergamo, Morelli, Ulmann and Berenson; Berlin, Bode, Van Marle, Yashiro;
Milan, L. and A. Venturi, Valentiner, Gamba, Mesnil, Berenson and
Salvini; Washington, Suida and Bettini.

18 Profile Portrait of a Woman. Panel, 40 × 61 cm. Florence,
Pitti. Both attribution and subject of this painting are controversial.
The traditional ascription to Botticelli is contested by Milanesi, Mo-
relli, Berenson and Yashiro, and favoured by Bode, Schmarsow, A.
Venturi, Van Marle, Gamba, L. Venturi, Mesnil, Bettini, Ciaranfi and
Salvini. It is dated by Salvini in the Pollaiolesque period, c. 1475.

19 Medici Adoration of the Magi. Detail: portrait of Lorenzo il
Magnifico (see *pl. 21*).

20 Medici Adoration of the Magi. Detail: portrait of Giuliano de'
Medici (see *pl. 21*).

21 Medici Adoration of the Magi. Panel, 134×111 cm. Florence,
Uffizi. The original attribution, now fully acknowledged, is from an
ancient source which also gives the picture's location as Santa Maria
Novella. The identification of the models is doubtful; the most likely
interpretations are: the first king kneeling in front of the Virgin,
Cosimo the Elder, the second and third, Piero the Gouty and Giovanni di Cosimo; the youth with the sword on the far left, Lorenzo
the Magnificent; the man in a yellow cape on the far right is
thought to be Botticelli. Ulmann sees a portrait of Lorenzo Tornabuoni in the young man wearing a feathered hat standing behind
Botticelli; Filippo Strozzi in the old man standing by the right hand
wall, and Agnolo Poliziano in the youth leaning on the shoulder of
Lorenzo the Magnificent. The painting can be dated about 1477.

22 Medici Adoration of the Magi. Detail: the peacock.

23 Medici Adoration of the Magi. Detail: Botticelli's self-portrait.

24 Madonna of the Sea. Panel, 28.5 × 40.5 cm. Florence, Uffizi. Formerly in the convent of Santa Felicità. Gamba's ascription to Botticelli is accepted by Procacci and Salvini; while Boeck, Berti and Baldini think it is by Filippino Lippi.

25 Madonna of the Sea. Detail: the head of the Virgin.

26 Spring. Detail: the three Graces (see *pl. 28*).

27 Spring. Detail: the three Graces (see *pl. 28*).

28 Spring. Panel, 314×203 cm. Florence, Uffizi. The work was executed for Lorenzo di Pierfrancesco and is mentioned in ancient sources as being in the Villa di Castello, which Pierfrancesco bought in 1477 (Horne). After Lorenzo's death the panel passed to Giovanni delle Bande Nere, and later to his son, Cosimo I. It is referred to as in the latter's possession by Vasari. It was moved into the Uffizi from Villa di Castello in 1815, then to the Accademia, and back to the Uffizi in 1919. The best interpretation of this allegory is undoubtedly Warburg's. This is a representation of the realm of Venus based on an idea of Poliziano's; on the right Zephyr pursues and holds Flora, Flora is transformed by Zephyr into the Hour of Spring, while Venus stands in the middle, with the three Graces and Mercury on her right. Other interpreters have seen in it an allegory of Simonetta's death and her rebirth in Elysium (Jacobsen); the marriage of a poet, in the person of Mercury, with a female satyr (Wickhoff), and Venus appearing at the judgment of Paris, as described by Apuleius (Gombrich). The interpretation by Battisti is interesting; a representation of the seasons, with the various months from February (Zephyr) to September (Mercury).

30 Spring. Detail: The Hour of Spring.

31 Spring. Detail: Flora.

32 Spring. Detail: Zephyr and Flora.

33 St Augustine in his Cell. Fresco, 112 × 152 cm. Florence, church of Ognissanti. Mentioned in ancient sources, particularly the Anonimo Gaddiano, who states that it was painted at the same time as Ghirlandaio's *St Jerome* (dated 1480). The date for this fresco is stylistically confirmed. Many experts have seen influences of Castagno in it.

33

34 Annunciation of San Martino alla Scala. Detached fresco, 550 ×243 cm. Florence, Belvedere, Mostra degli affreschi. Detail of the angel. This fresco originally decorated the loggia of the hospital of San Martino alla Scala, which later became the entrance hall of the church of the same name. The fresco was detached about 1920. Poggi's research gives further evidence to support the view that this work was painted by Sandro between April and May 1481, shortly before he went to Rome.

35 Annunciation of San Martino alla Scala. Detail: the Virgin.

36 Madonna Adoring the Child with Infant St John. Panel, tondo, diameter 95 cm. Piacenza, Museo Civico. It is not accepted as an entirely authentic work by the majority of critics (exceptions are Gamba and Mesnil). I support the suggestion that it was painted in collaboration about 1481.

37 Temptation of Christ. Fresco, 115 × 345.5 cm. Rome, Sistine Chapel. Landscape detail. The decoration ' *affresco* ' of the Sistine Chapel was assigned to Botticelli, Ghirlandaio, Perugino and Cosimo Rosselli by Pope Sixtus IV in 1481. It is assumed that by 27 October of that year (document published by Gnoli) each painter had completed one fresco, as the full payment for the commission was to be assessed on the work executed by that date. Ten stories from the Old Testament had still to be painted for the completion of the cycle by 15 March 1482. As the number of frescoes required had been increased, three more painters were brought in to help with the work, Pinturicchio, Signorelli and Piero di Cosimo. The subject of this series of frescoes is taken from parallel stories from the Old and New Testament.

38 Temptation of Christ. Detail: group of onlookers. The ecclesiastic facing outwards is thought to be either Raffaello Riario or Giuliano della Rovere, both nephews of the Pope.

39 Temptation of Christ. Detail: the girl carrying wood.

40 Abundance. Drawing (black pencil, pen and watercolour, touched with white on reddish prepared paper), 25.3 × 31.7 cm. London, British Museum. The attribution to Botticelli by Ulmann is fully accepted. Can be dated after his stay in Rome, about 1482.

41 Pallas and the Centaur. Canvas, 148×207 cm. Florence, Uffizi. Discovered by Ridolfi in a corridor of the Palazzo Pitti, and removed to the Uffizi in 1922. It belonged with the *Spring* to Lorenzo di Pierfrancesco, and was later inherited by Giovanni delle Bande Nere. The allegorical theme has been interpreted in various ways: Ridolfi sees in it the victory of Lorenzo the Magnificent (Pallas representing wisdom) over the court of Naples (the Centaur), and dates it around 1480, immediately after Lorenzo's return from

Naples; Steinmann believes it to symbolize the supremacy of the Medici over the Pazzi; Frothingham, the political balance of power maintained by Lorenzo; Wittkower (very plausibly) the union of wisdom and instinct in the person of Lorenzo, whose device (three diamond rings) is embroidered on Pallas' dress. Perhaps the most acceptable explanation of all is by Gombrich, who traces its meaning to Ficino, whose philosophy was an inspiration for the *Spring*: according to this view the Centaur represents both the sensual side of man (the animal part), and his reason (the human part), subdued by wisdom (Minerva). Berenson agrees with Ridolfi and Yashiro on the date 1480; both Horne and L. Venturi date it 1488, (supposing it to refer to the alliance between Lorenzo and Innocent VIII formed in 1487), while Bode suggests the year 1485, on which Mesnil and Bettini agree. The most reliable date is probably 1482-3, given by A. Venturi, Van Marle, Gamba and Salvini.

42 Lorenzo Tornabuoni Presented to the Seven Liberal Arts.
Detached fresco, 269×227 cm. Paris, Louvre. This fresco, with the one below (*pl. 43*), was originally a loggia decoration for a villa belonging to Tornabuoni, near Careggi, later bought by the Lemmi family. The attribution to Botticelli, now universally accepted, stems from Cavalcaselle. The young man in the fresco has been identified as Lorenzo Tornabuoni, who was executed in 1497 after taking part in a plot to secure the return of Piero dei Medici. The girl in the companion fresco is believed to be Giovanna degli Albizi The identification of Tornabuoni is probably correct, but the girl's identity seems doubtful; the coat of arms near the girl is not that of the Albizi family, while the girl's features differ from those in Ghirlandaio's portrait of her in his *Visitation* in Santa Maria Novella, and in that of the medal by Nicolò Fiorentino. As the Albizi coat of arms has been added in tempera to the first fresco, Salvini reasonably concludes ' this addition was painted at the time of the wedding in 1486, so that both frescoes, originally painted for another occasion, would be associated with the Tornabuoni-Albizi marriage '. Hence the necessity to date this work before 1486. Both frescoes are also in the style of that period.

43 Venus Followed by Graces Offers Gifts to a Girl. Detached fresco, 284 × 212 cm. Paris, Louvre.

44 Venus Followed by Graces Offers Gifts to a Girl. Detail: the Graces.

45 Venus Followed by Graces Offers Gifts to a Girl. Detail of the girl.

46 Second Panel of the Story of Nastagio degli Onesti. Panel, 112×84 cm. Madrid, Prado. Detail. This panel and its companion (*pl. 47*) belong to a group of four which illustrate a tale from Boccaccio. Attributed to Botticelli by Vasari. According to recent critics the design is by Botticelli, but the work was executed by studio assistants. The presence of the coats of arms of the Pucci and Bini families has led Horne to assume that the panels were executed in 1483 for the wedding of Giannozzo Pucci and Lucrezia Bini.

47 Third Panel of the Story of Nastagio degli Onesti. Panel, 112 × 84 cm. Prado, Madrid. Detail.

48 Madonna of the Magnificat. Panel, tondo, diameter 118 cm. Florence, Uffizi. Much repainted, mostly in the faces of the Virgin and Child. Considered an early work by Cavalcaselle, it has since been variously dated by modern critics: Ulmann, Horne, A. Venturi, Gamba, Argan and Salvini suggest a date about 1482, Yashiro and Van Marle agree on 1481, before the artist's journey to Rome, while Bode, followed by Schmarsow, Venturi and Bettini, favours the year 1485.

49 Madonna of the Magnificat. Detail of the Virgin.

50 Madonna and Child. Panel, 39.5 × 58 cm. Milan, Museo Poldi Pezzoli. It is universally acknowledged as an authentic work, and is generally agreed to have been painted more or less at the same time as the *Madonna of the Magnificat*.

51 Madonna and Child. Detail of the Child (see *pl. 51*).

52 Venus and Mars. Panel, 173.5 × 69 cm. London, National Gallery. Ulmann, followed by most critics, dates it around 1485-6, immediately after the *Birth of Venus*, while Bode and Van Marle believe it was painted in 1476-8; Schmarsow, with whom Argan agrees, dates it back to 1475. Salvini maintains it was painted shortly before the *Birth of Venus*, in 1483. Here again, we turn to Gombrich for the interpretation of the subject as an idea derived from Ficino (the influence of Venus, seen as *humanitas*, on Mars the symbol of war).

53 Birth of Venus. Detail: Venus (see *pl. 55*).

54 Birth of Venus. Detail of Hour (see *pl. 55*).

55 Birth of Venus. Canvas, 278.5 × 172.5 cm. Florence, Uffizi. Its presence in the Villa del Castello suggests that it was painted for Lorenzo di Pierfrancesco. Later it became the property of Giovanni delle Bande Nere and finally of Cosimo I. Its date is a matter of some controversy: Bode suggests 1478; Ulmann, followed by Horne, A. Venturi, Gamba, L. Venturi, Bettini and Argan, thinks it was painted in 1485-6; Yashiro in 1487, Van Marle in 1481-2, Salvini in 1484. The subject of the painting is evidently inspired by the Homeric hymn to Venus, by the stanzas of Poliziano, and partly by Ovid. Wickhoff thought it represented the arrival of Venus in Sicily, as narrated in the *Pervigilium Veneris*. Here too, the most reliable analysis is by Gombrich, who mentions Ficino's and Pico della Mirandola's interpretations of the Birth of Venus as narrated by Hesiod (the goddess was generated from the testicles of Uranus, castrated by Chronos and cast into the sea). This story was interpreted as the birth of Beauty from the union of Idea and Matter.

56 Madonna of the Pomegranate. Panel, tondo, diameter 143.5 cm. Florence, Uffizi. Horne (followed by A. Venturi, Gamba, Bettini and Salvini) believes that this tondo should be identified with one which Botticelli painted in 1487 for the court-room of the Magistrato dei Massai in the Palazzo Vecchio. This hypothesis seems to be supported by the frame, decorated with a frieze of lilies. But this identification and dating of the tondo is not shared by Ulmann (who suggests a date previous to 1480), Bode, Schmarsow, Yashiro, L. Venturi (*c.* 1482), Berenson, Mesnil or Van Marle.

57 Madonna of the Pomegranate. Detail of the Virgin.

58 San Barnaba Altarpiece. Panel, 280 × 268 cm. Florence, Uffizi. Painted for the convent of San Barnaba, it was moved to the Accademia when the convent was closed, and later to the Uffizi. It represents the Madonna and Child on a throne with four angels and Saints Catherine of Alexandria, Augustine, Barnabas, John the Baptist, Ignatius and Michael the Archangel. Mentioned in early sources (Albertini, Antonio Bini, Vasari). Dates vary from 1480 to 1494. Il was probably painted as Salvini suggests, c. 1488. Ulmann dates it 1480, Horne, Bode, Schmarsow, Yashiro, L. and A. Venturi in 1482-3; Gamba, Bettini and Argan suggest it was begun 1487 and completed some years later.

59 San Barnaba Altarpiece. Detail of St John the Baptist, St Ignatius and St Michael the Archangel.

60 Annunciation. Panel, 156 × 150 cm. Florence, Uffizi. Cited by Vasari as an authentic work and located by him in the church of Santa Maria Maddalena dei Pazzi. Documents found by Milanesi suggest that the panel was executed between 1489 and 1490. Its authenticity is acknowledged by Ulmann, Bode, A. and L. Venturi, Mesnil and Salvini; it is attributed to Sandro's studio by Morelli, Yashiro, Van Marle, Berenson, Gamba and Bettini.

61 Annunciation. Detail of landscape.

62 Madonna and Child with Young St John. Panel, 73.5 × 89.5 cm. Dresden, Gemäldegalerie. Accepted as Botticelli's unaided work by some critics (Morelli, Gamba and Salvini). Ulmann, A. Venturi, Berenson and Mesnil among others consider it a studio work, painted towards the end of 1490.

63 Annunciation. Panel, 36 × 24 cm. New York, Lehman Collection. Acknowledged as Botticelli's work by Ulmann, Bode, Schmarsow, Van Marle, Yashiro, L. Venturi, Gamba, Salvini; dates vary from

1474 to after 1500. Attributed to the school of Botticelli by Morelli, Horne and A. Venturi. I agree with Bode, who dates this predella panel between 1485 and 1490.

64 St Augustine in his Cell. Panel, 27 × 41 cm. Florence, Uffizi. Morelli's attribution is accepted, though dates vary from about 1490 (Ulmann, Horne, Bode, Van Marle and Salvini) to 1495 (A. Venturi, Gamba) and 1500 (Yashiro, Bettini).

65 Nativity. Pen and watercolour touched with white on prepared paper, 26 × 16 cm. Florence, Uffizi. Unanimously attributed to Sandro, and dated 1491 (Yashiro).

66 Lamentation. Panel, 207 × 110 cm. Munich, Alte Pinakothek. Formerly in the church of San Paolino, bought in 1815 for King Ludwig of Bavaria. Acknowledged as autograph by Cavalcaselle, Ulmann, Morelli, Bode, Schmarsow, A. and L. Venturi, Gamba, Mesnil, Bettini, Argan and Salvini, as a workshop painting by Berenson, Horne, Van Marle. Date of execution c. 1490.

67 Lamentation. Panel, 71 × 107 cm. Milan, Museo Poldi Pezzoli. Some critics think this is the panel mentioned by Vasari in Santa Maria Maggiore (identified by others with the Munich *Lamentation, pl. 66*). Other believe both *Lamentations* are versions of the *Pietà* in Santa Maria Maggiore (Horne). The ascription to Botticelli is favoured by Ulmann, Bode, Schmarsow, Van Marle, Gamba, Bettini, Argan and Salvini. May be dated, like the Munich *Lamentation*, to the last decade of the fifteenth century.

68 Drawing for Canto XXXIII of Dante's Purgatorio. 32 × 47 cm. Formerly in Berlin, Kupferstichkabinett. Botticelli illustrated the *Commedia* for Lorenzo di Pierfrancesco (Anonimo Gaddiano). These drawings have been identified as those found in a codex in the Hamilton Library, which was bought in Paris in 1803, then transferred in its entirety to the Berlin Museum in 1882. Some of the missing pages of the Hamilton codex were found in a miscellaneous one in the Vatican. Each folio contained one Canto set out in four columns on the recto, and a drawing illustrating the following Canto on the verso. These lead and silverpoint drawings were meant to be coloured. The Vatican Library owns the plan of the *Inferno*, which has an illustration for Canto I of the *Inferno* on the back, and also drawings for Cantos IX, X, XII, XIII, XV, XVI; while in Berlin, prior to the second world war, drawings existed for Canto VIII and XVII-XXXIV of the *Inferno* as well as all the *Purgatorio* and *Paradiso* drawings, except XXX and XXXIII of the *Paradiso*. Unfortunately, nearly all the Berlin sheets were dispersed during the war. Only three drawings (*Inferno* XXIX and XXXI, and *Purgatorio* III) are now to be found in the Staatliche Museen in Berlin. All are universally accepted as authentic; the date must be related to the political events, between 1490-6, affecting the career of Lorenzo di Pierfrancesco, by whom these works were commissioned.

69 Drawing for Canto XXIX of the Paradiso. 32 × 47 cm. Formerly in Berlin, Kupferstichkabinett.

70 Calumny. Panel, 91 × 62 cm. Florence, Galleria degli Uffizi. Mentioned by Vasari as being in the house of Fabio Segni. The subject is derived from a famous painting by Apelles, described in Lucian's *De Calumnia*, which Botticelli presumably read in a Latin translation either by Guarino Veronese or Fontio (1472), or else in the Florentine edition of 1496. Lucian's description is also paraphrased by Alberti (*De Pictura*, 1434). The allegory represents a youth carried away by Calumny, who is accompanied by Deceit and Fraud, and brought into the presence of King Midas, beside whom stand Ignorance and Suspicion. Near Calumny stands Penitence, an old woman, and, on the left side of the painting, a naked girl represents Truth. The date of this work is generally placed in the last decade of the century.

71 Calumny. Detail: Truth.

72 Calumny. Detail: Penitence.

73 Story of Virginia. Panel, 165 × 86 cm. Bergamo, Accademia Carrara. Ascribed to Botticelli by Morelli. It has been identified as one of the panel paintings mentioned by Vasari, and located by him in Giovanni Vespucci's house. All critics agree on the ascription and dating of the work in the last decade of the century.

74 Mystic Nativity. Canvas, 75 × 108.5 cm. London, National Gallery. It has been in the National Gallery since 1878. It was brought to England from Rome at the end of the eighteenth century, and found its way into various English collections. In the upper part of the painting there is a Greek epigraph which can be translated as follows: ' I Sandro painted this picture at the end of year 1500 [i.e. early in 1501] in the troubles of Italy in the mid-time after the time according to the 11th chapter of St John in the second woe of the Apocalypse in the loosing of the devil for three and a half years then he will be chained in the 12th chapter and we shall see clearly ... as in this picture.' It is commonly accepted that this canvas represents the prophesy of Liberation (the birth of Christ as a triumph of the divine world) from the reign of the Antichrist, who manifested himself through the disorders in Italy to which this inscription refers, and in the death of Savonarola.

1

2

3

4

6

7

8

9

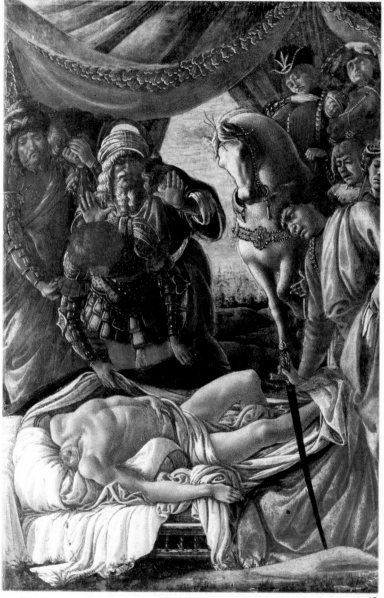

15

18

31

41

51

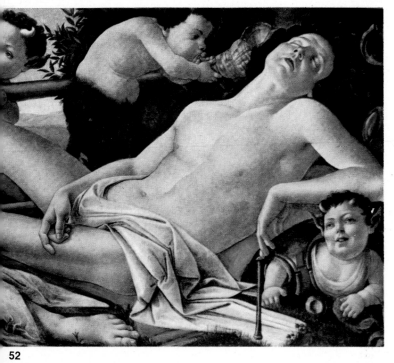

53

57

58

61

64

67